THE BARON A...
ARTIST

He was the Baro...
He was the man...
taking risks which...
sometimes giving chase to criminals, as he
was now, sometimes on the run from the
police who had often been close on his heels.
Then, he had been jewel-thief extraordinary,
cracksman, and also a kind of Robin Hood,
robbing the rich to help the poor. Further back,
long years back, he had been a thief both for
the thrill and for the gain, robbing only the
wealthy and yet on the wrong side of the law
and for a few brief years, making his living
from his daring thefts.
It was like a vivid series of flashbacks.
The excitement and the danger had brought
them to him; but if he slipped he would roll
down the roof and crash, breaking bones
even if he did not kill himself.

The Baron and the Arrogant Artist

John Creasey
as Anthony Morton

CORONET BOOKS
Hodder Paperbacks Ltd., London

Printed and bound in Great Britain for
Coronet Books, Hodder Paperbacks Ltd,
St. Paul's House, Warwick Lane,
London EC4P 4AH
By C. Nicholls & Company Ltd.,
The Philips Park Press, Manchester.

ISBN 0 340 18763 8

CONTENTS

I

The Young Couple

"OH, TOM," THE GIRL pleaded. "Don't, please don't."

"Of course I'm going to tackle him," said the young man, angrily. "Parasites like Mannering owe the world something."

Quick as a shot, the girl retorted:

"But you're not the world! Even if he is a parasite, he doesn't owe *you* anything."

And, that said, the young man and the young woman stared at each other, in fact glared at each other, in Hart Row, Mayfair, outside the far-famed shop named Quinns. They were, as becomes, or at least is common to the young, absorbed only in themselves. Neither was the world, but to each there were times when the world seemed empty but for them, as it did now.

They did not realise that they were being observed by three pairs of interested eyes.

And they did not realise that every whispered and muted word, even their heavy breathing, could be heard inside the shop. For the gilded Old English lettering above the dark oak fascia of Quinns concealed two microphones which, when alive, picked up all the sounds from outside the window. Usually these sounds were muted for the loudspeakers in the long, narrow, shadowy shop were turned low, but one of the assistants always listened and, when the talk outside seemed to concern Quinns, turned up the volume and switched on other loudspeakers.

A young man in his early twenties stood by the microphone control at the back of the shop, concealed by a partition of beautifully carved oak, once the head panel of the bed of an Italian prince; in the carving there were several holes through which the whole shop could be surveyed, with all its treasures. At one side, moving a polishing cloth gently, even lovingly, over a Regency walnut chest, was another young man; both of these, in pale grey suits of Edwardian cut had a touch of elegance very different from the appearance of the now-angry youth outside the window.

In the doorway of an office across a narrow passageway from the dead prince's bed panel a third man stood, listened and stared. He was William Bristow, a grey-haired, fit-looking man in his late fifties, not long since one of Britain's leading policemen and now the manager of Quinns. He had been about to leave the office of the owner of Quinns — one John Mannering — as the couple had started talking and, in his wisdom, the youth had turned up the volume, Bristow now stood with his fingers on the handle of Mannering's door.

Mannering could hear but not see.

A remarkably handsome man who seemed ageless but was in fact in the middle-to-late-forties, he sat at a bow-fronted Queen Anne desk, behind books and files and telephones, smiling faintly, even sardonically. For it was he who was being called a parasite.

All who watched and all who listened now waited for the effect of the girl's 'You're not the world'. This had been very sharp and the young man with her held his breath as if he knew that whatever he wanted to say, he must control it.

At last, he answered: "I am going to see him. He makes a fat living out of art and artists, and indirectly he owes a lot to all artists. But—" he now drew back, raising his hands with a dramatic gesture. "You don't have to come. You don't have to stay here. You don't even have to see me again."

He spun round towards the shop door.

By this time Mannering had become so curious that he joined Bristow at the door and looked towards the window. In it was a single painting, an English landscape by Constable, and the window was cunningly lighted so that the glow reflected on people looking in at the window : for often a man or woman's expression when outside gave a clue to the individual's intentions, even though a mask seemed to fall over their faces whenever they came inside. This young man's face was sharp-featured, his dark hair long, his lips set. The girl, who was golden-haired, petite and shapely in mini skirt and black bolero, looked less hurt than sad, and her voice was very clear.

"If you go in and bother Mr. Mannering or anyone in the shop you won't see me again, Tom." And after the briefest of pauses, she went on : "I mean it."

He turned away from her and pushed the door open and stepped inside.

"Bill," murmured Mannering, "nip out and see where the girl goes, will you?"

"Right." Bristow's reflexes were as good as those of most young men, and he turned towards the rear of the shop, a hallway and the back door. Mannering heard that click shut as he himself stepped into the shop. The young man on duty at the amplifier switched off as the stranger entered by the front door, while the other assistant stepped forward from the fifteenth century chest he had been polishing to accost the newcomer. Outside, the girl peered in for a moment, then turned and disappeared.

"Good morning," said the Edwardian-clad young man, who had between-coloured hair so immaculate that it might have been a wig, and a complexion so perfect that it might have been a woman's. "May I help you?"

"I want to see John Mannering," declared the stranger.

There was much arrogance in him; and there was pride. Closer at hand he had something of the look of a hawk, and his grey eyes something of a hawk's brightness. His dark hair was coarse but groomed and clean. He wore a lambskin bolero-type jacket over a vivid blue shirt, and tight-fitting Levis, while his brass-studded shoes had high heels built far under the instep.

"I am afraid Mr. Mannering sees callers only by appointment," replied the Edwardian exquisite in his beautifully modulated voice. "And he is not free today."

"He's here and he's free," rasped the caller. "And you know it."

"Indeed," said the exquisite, whose name was Rupert Smith. "If you will leave your name —"

The caller growled : "My name is Forrester," and as he spoke he moved forward swiftly, obviously intending to push past Rupert Smith.

Mannering, now behind the royal screen, saw everything with graphic clarity.

The long, narrow shop; the furniture and pictures and show-cases containing jewellery, the pictures on the panelled walls, the miniatures, the china and porcelain : each in its way was a treasure. The passage running down the middle of the shop was clearly defined with deep red carpet. There were little recesses, or bays, on either side in which one could get closer to anything of especial interest. There was no room for two people to pass at the middle aisle unless one or the other stepped aside; and the man who had introduced himself as Forrester obviously expected the dandy to do so.

Rupert Smith did no such thing.

Mannering, quick to observe danger signals, saw the two lithe young bodies tense; saw arms bend, swift movement without fuss; in a way they were like fighting cocks. The assistant close to Mannering drew in a hissing breath and stepped towards the passage but Mannering put out a detaining hand. In the heart of the shop the two men were at grips, but neither spoke. It was as if each saw the other as an adversary with whom there must inevitably be a trial of strength. The young faces grew tense and pale. Two pairs of eyes narrowed, two pairs of lips set tight. Neither of them appeared to breathe but both began to sway in unison.

There was a gasp.

Suddenly, Forrester went hurtling back, losing his balance. With quite startling speed Rupert Smith passed him, reached the door, pulled it open until it was caught by a floor-catch, spun round in time to seize Forrester's right arm and to hoist it up behind his back in a hammer-lock. Instantly, he spun the other round and thrust him towards the street. There had been scarcely time to realise what was happening but now Mannering saw Bristow close to Quinns front door.

Bristow asked clearly: "What's all this?"

Mannering did not wait to hear more but turned and followed the route which Bristow had taken. Clear fluor-escent light shone on the panelled walls, a narrow, twisting Jacobean staircase, the wall of which was beamed with oak hundreds of years old. He went out in an alley-way, which stopped just beyond Quinns on the left at a reinforced concrete wall of a mammoth office block, and ran into Hart Row at the other end It was only a few steps, and he ran until he saw the fair-haired girl standing in a shop doorway on the other side of Hart Row. She did not see him, she was so intent on what was happening at the front entrance to Quinns.

Mannering turned the corner.

Bristow was standing on one side. Forrester was on the pavement, with Rupert Smith blocking the doorway. Several people were in the narrow street, two of them glancing over at the three men. As he approached, Man-nering heard Bristow say sharply:

"That's enough, unless you want us to fetch the police."

"Police," sneered Forrester. "All they're for is to defend you and your bloody kind."

"Mr. Bristow," interrupted Rupert with great delibera-tion, "told you you had said enough."

Forrester glared. His face was pasty white, his thin body at great tension. Now Mannering could see that his cheeks were hollow and he had not only a lean but a hungry look. His hands were tightly clenched, and he began to speak

again. Before he uttered more than a growling "I" the girl
passed Mannering, light-footed, swift, graceful, and she
stood in front of Forrester, speaking in a low-pitched but
authoritative voice. Mannering noticed that her golden
hair was brushed and clean, but her mini-skirt was loose
and her stockings had huge ladders. Her black, much em-
broidered bolero, was much too big for her.

"Tom, let's get away at once." She took his arm and
pulled, and although he resisted it was only token resistance, for immediately he began to follow her.

Mannering was quite sure that he saw tears of vexation
in his eyes.

He, Mannering, said in his most casual, friendly voice :

"Hallo, Bill. Am I too late for something?"

The young caller spun round. The girl dropped his arm.
Bristow was taken completely by surprise, while Rupert
Smith spoke with admirable composure.

"Good morning, sir. I didn't realise you would be back
so soon. I told this gentleman you could only see callers by
appointment."

After a pause while he smiled at both Forrester and the
girl, Mannering said : "Well usually that's true enough,
but there's no one else waiting for me, is there?"

Bristow was slightly slow on the uptake.

"Er — no, John, there isn't."

"Then if it won't take too long, and as he's here, let's go
into my office," said Mannering, and he stood aside for
both young man and girl to pass.

She was staring at him with an expression of overwhelming gratitude; her eyes were actually moist. The
bolero was fresh and clean but patched; so was a dark
green blouse she wore beneath it; even the brown tweed
mini-skirt was both frayed and patched. She had a rather
broad nose, up-tilted, and nice green-grey eyes, free from
eye-shading, and a fresh but undoubtedly hungry look; too
thin despite the grace with which she moved. Suddenly
the shop was crowded and Mannering took the girl's arm
to make room for them to walk side by side, while he

called to Jonathan Armitage, the other Edwardian exquisite.

"Will you make some coffee and bring some biscuits, Jon? I missed breakfast." That was as white a lie as he had told for a long time. He opened the door of his office and ushered the couple in, while Bristow hovered, meaningfully. This office was also the entrance to Mannering's strong room, which was approached through a large opening in the floor covered, at the moment, by a winged armchair. Mannering had no fears about this couple but ex-Chief Detective Superintendent Bristow, so recently of New Scotland Yard, took nothing for granted. He came in and pushed up chairs for the young couple while Mannering offered cigarettes, which both refused.

Tom Forrester had the grace to look ill-at-ease, whereas the girl sat back with a sigh of relief; she wasn't exactly beautiful but if her cheeks had been a little fuller and if she were even lightly made-up, she would be most provocatively attractive.

Bristow went out, leaving the door ajar, for at Mannering's foot was a push which would raise instant alarm if there were any cause. Now Mannering sat back in a swivel chair, the only contemporary piece of furniture here, and looked from the boy to the girl. At close quarters Forrester was undoubtedly little more than a boy.

"Well —" Mannering began.

"Mr. Mannering —" said the girl.

"It's so bloody unfair!" burst out Tom Forrester.

"Oh, *Tom*," breathed the girl. "Tom, *don't*, please."

"But it is!" cried Forrester. "And you know it is! The fact that Mannering's been damned decent doesn't make it just, you know it as well as I do!" His voice was low-pitched and aquiver and his lips were quivering, too.

He had a huge, unwieldy chip on his shoulder, and that wasn't unique among the youth of the day. The girl had such a steady courage, and that wasn't unusual either. Now she looked at Forrester in acute vexation, one hand raised as if she could slap him.

"Is anything just?" asked Mannering lightly. "Or isn't it mostly the luck of the draw?" He leaned forward and went on earnestly : "I don't mean to be flippant, I really mean that seriously."

"Oh, it *is* luck !" cried the girl.

"Then all I can say is that you've been damned lucky, Man — Mr. Mannering."

"Ah," said Mannering, eyeing Forrester levelly. "I suppose that's true. If it is really luck to have elementary good manners. I wonder if you realise how insufferably rude you've been since you came into this office?"

Forrester jerked upright, obviously astounded. At first the girl was startled but she soon relaxed, a smile playing about her lips. They sat in silence for at least half-a-minute, before Forrester leaned back in his chair and said : "I'm sorry," in a gruff voice.

On that instant, as if it were a cue, the door opened wider and Jonathan Armitage came in carrying a tray with coffee, cream and sugar and a dish piled high with biscuits in several varieties. The gaze of both girl and youth turned towards this plenitude as if the effect were mesmeric, and Mannering had no doubt that both were famished. So as soon as the tray was on the desk he held out the biscuits for the girl to take and busied himself asking 'black?' or 'white?' or 'do you take sugar?' while they took biscuits and tried not to gobble them down. It was astonishing how quickly they relaxed and how soon colour came into their cheeks and a glow in their eyes. When a telephone call came from another London dealer Mannering dragged it out so that the biscuits could be devoured without his noticing; when he had finished there were just four left, one of each variety.

He poured out more coffee for them and himself, remembered his story of missing breakfast and ate the remaining biscuits : enough was enough. At last, looking from one to the other, he asked :

"Well now — what is it you think I can do to make life a little fairer?"

They were both taken aback again, but after a moment Forrester actually laughed at this mild joke against himself. Soon his sober and earnest mood returned, and he started to speak. But the girl spoke first, silencing him.

"Tom is an artist," she stated. "A painter. And — well, he desperately needs some commissions, or a job to keep him going while he paints."

Before Mannering could ask how he was expected to help, while the girl placed a small but shapely hand on Forrester's knee as if to urge 'Keep quiet', the young man spoke with great precision, obviously determined that there should be not the slightest doubt or misunderstanding.

"I am potentially a very great artist indeed," he declared. "And I do not want a time-wasting job. I need a stake — a patron — who will give me a year or even two or three, while the art world begins to understand and value my work. *That's* what I need, Mr. Mannering. And as you make a fortune out of art, including paintings, I decided to give you the chance."

As he finished his head was high with a kind of pride that most people would have regarded as arrogance.

The girl, lips quivering and eyes misted, turned her face away.

2

Good, Bad or Indifferent

IT WAS A CURIOUS fact, but Mannering became aware of the girl only on the perimeter of his mind yet was acutely aware of the young man. Coming from most people his attitude, his challenge, would have been simply rude, or brash, or big-headed. And it was each of these. Yet there was something beyond them. Tension showed at Forrester's lips, which were so beautifully-formed that they looked as if they were carved. His hollow cheeks and pointed, bony chin heightened the impression that he was hungry-thin, but it was the eyes, grey, fierce looking, deep-set beneath jutting eyebrows, which made him look out of the ordinary: a predator. His hair grew far back from his forehead but left a prominent widow's peak, like an arrow pointing from his forehead to his hawked nose.

All of these things took time to assess; during that time Thomas Forrester did not shift his gaze, and colour came slowly to his cheeks. The girl now watched Mannering, a puzzled expression on her face, as if she could not understand why he had not simply told her Tom that he had no time nor patience with him.

At last, Mannering smiled faintly.

"You mean that I should be proud to sponsor you, as a patron of the arts, not that I should invest in you as a possible up and coming artist who could one day make me money?"

"I didn't say that." Forrester's lips seemed dry and he had some difficulty in getting the words out. "I think you

— well, *someone*, should sponsor me and take a chance whether he ever gets his money back."

"Why you?" asked Mannering, when the others had been poised for 'Why me?'.

The girl now sat upright, eagerness in her eyes, body poised. Forrester was momentarily taken aback, but for the first time a gleam as of humour shone in his eyes. It softened and humanised him.

"Because I'm good."

"How can you prove it?"

"I've hundreds of paintings which will."

"Where are they?"

"In my —" Forrester hesitated, glanced at the girl and said : "In Julie's flat."

"Where's that?"

"In Fulham — and *not* the fashionable part."

"How many of the paintings have you sold?" inquired Mannering, not slackening the pressure of his question one iota.

Forrester drew in a hissing breath.

"None. But that doesn't mean —"

"It means that so far the paintings aren't saleable, unless —" Mannering's voice sharpened : "You haven't tried to sell them."

"*Tried*," breathed Forrester. "We've done everything short of going down on our knees and *begging* someone to buy one. There was one foul dealer who said he would buy one every time Julie went to bed with him; that's as near as I ever got to a sale."

Now his face had become alabaster pale, his lips quivered, his eyes were glittering.

"What did you do to him?" asked Mannering, interestedly.

"I knocked him down."

"I see," said Mannering, as if approvingly. "But —" he looked at Julie with a smile — "in this day and age, as I understand it, a lot of young people don't believe in a one man, one woman society."

"In this day and age," reported Forrester thinly, "the generation gap is almost unbridgeable. If you think I'm a pimp who will live off money Julie earns with her body — my *God*. I ought to smash your face in!"

"*Tom*," breathed Julie, speaking for the first time since Mannering had started his questions.

"So you are an upright young man full of great moral scruples," Mannering said drily. "How old are you, Mr. Forrester?"

"I'm twenty-three. What the hell has that got to do with you?"

"If I'm to support you I need to know." When Forrester didn't answer, Mannering went on: "Have you ever earned a living?"

"I — yes."

"For how long?"

"I — my God! I don't have to answer these questions."

"When you came here and asked for my sponsorship you laid yourself open to these questions," Mannering pointed out.

"They're wholly irrelevant!"

"Then let me make them relevant. I need to know how old you are and I need to know for what proportion of your adult life you've supported yourself and for how much of it you've been supported by others. Am I your first sponsor-to-be? Or has there been a string of them?"

This time the spate of questions seemed to engulf Forrester, and to subdue if not to crush him. For the first time he looked away from Mannering, and then slowly turned to Julie and at the same time began to get up. In a dull voice, he said:

"Come on. Let's go."

"Tom —"

Forrester stood upright, and put a hand on her shoulder.

"I said let's go," he repeated in a manner which held all the arrogance he had shown at the beginning of the visit. Now he seemed to be exerting not simply control over the girl, but ownership; whatever he said, Julie must do.

For a few seconds, Julie sat as if undecided. She did not attempt to get up. She glanced from Forrester and back to Mannering, a frown wrinkling her smooth, broad forehead. Still without moving, she asked:

"Mr. Mannering, are you considering Tom's proposition?"

"Of course." Mannering answered.

"You're going a bloody funny way about it," growled Forrester.

"You are a bloody difficult man to deal with," replied Mannering in the pleasantest of voices. "I haven't seen any of your work but if you've so many pictures you must be dedicated to painting, and if Julie remains so ardently loyal and full of faith there must be more of a man as well as a painter in you than I can see from the outside." He paused long enough for Forrester to reply but the youth seemed so surprised that he couldn't find words. So Mannering went on: "Have you had other sponsors?"

"No," growled Forrester. He gulped, and then went on: "I inherited enough from my father to keep going for five years. For the last year, Julie's kept me."

She started up. "Tom —"

"Well, I have lived on you," Forrester growled, and he turned back to Mannering, placed his hands on the desk and leaned forward so that their faces were almost level and only a foot apart. "*And* I've lived with her out of wedlock. Does *that* shock your conventional soul?"

For the first time since they had been here, Mannering was angry — very angry indeed with this young man who used the girl as a weapon with which to strike out to hurt, ignoring the fact that in doing so he hurt her. But Mannering did not respond in anger. That was not only for the girl's sake; it was perhaps a kind of sixth-sense, probably no more than a kind of commonsense, which told him that this youth might have a touch of genius; and genius was rare indeed.

At last, he said: "Yes, Forrester. It shocks me that you should tell a stranger that. But I am not interested in your domestic life or the moralities. I'm not even interested in whether you are an unpleasant or an aggressive young man. I am interested in whether you can paint, whether you have the spark. Most men of genius go through periods when they are utterly odious."

Forrester breathed: "My God! I could break your neck!" He grabbed Julie's arm again and pulled, and this time she didn't resist: it was almost as if she knew that there could be no reasoning with Tom; no hope at all. So, she went out with him. Mannering pressed a button on his desk and the door opened mechanically. He moved to the passage, but there was no need to follow, for Forrester was striding ahead, Julie some feet behind him. She had long, shapely legs which drew the gaze of both Armitage and Rupert Smith.

Bristow emerged from behind the bench covered by the partition.

"Did you hear that?" Mannering asked.

"Yes. And odious was the word," Bristow agreed heartily.

"It certainly drove him out," Mannering observed. "So he's really sensitive on one spot. Bring the tape in, will you? I'd like to hear that fascinating conversation over again."

Bristow picked up a small battery-type tape-recorder and went into the office with it. The recorder had been switched on and the conversation had been taped as Bristow had listened-in at a muted loudspeaker. Mannering could have switched this off from his office but had wanted the recording made, as he did nine out of ten interviews in the office. It was a much better way of recording a business conversation than making notes or having a short-hand typist present.

In one corner of the shop a cupboard with a door of carved oak panelling contained thousands of these recordings, while other files in his office and behind the partition had been transcribed, and copies were in fire-proof filing cabinets.

Bristow plugged the machine into a socket attached to the desk as Mannering sat on a corner of the table. Every word came through clearly, even every nuance; and when it was finished, Bristow said grimly :

"A nasty piece of work."

"A nasty show of manners," Mannering remarked. "And a lot of desperation."

"He's driven himself to it."

"Oh, I know, I know," Mannering said. "Is it any less painful if you put the thorns on your own head?"

Bristow, his face so clean-cut, his clipped moustache stained brown with nicotine, wearing a white gardenia in the left-side lapel of his pale grey suit; unplugged the recorder and took out the tape.

"I could feel sorry for the girl," he said, "but not for that young oaf."

Frowning, Mannering said : "I hope I didn't drive him too far."

Bristow gave a half-laugh, and remarked : "You couldn't. No one could."

Then a telephone call came from a Roman dealer who was visiting London and who said that he had some Michelangelo cartoons which might interest Mannering. They were on view in Rome, if he, Mannering, could combine other visits to the continent with a look at the cartoons it might be to his very great advantage. Mannering promised to ring back. Almost at once another call came, this time from a senior officer at New Scotland Yard.

"Sorry to worry you, Mr. Mannering, but do you think you could spare Bill Bristow for a couple of hours this afternoon?"

"I'm sure I can," responded Mannering. "Whether he'll want to come is another matter ! I'll put you through." He switched the telephone to Bristow, had a swift mental image of Julie, whose surname he didn't know, and of Tom Forrester. Bristow had no time at all for Forrester and it certainly looked as if he had made a most uncomfortable bed for himself, but there was still a spark of interest in

Mannering's mind. Before long, Bristow tapped at the door and, when he came in, looked excited.

"They want you back at the Yard," hazarded Mannering.

"Just for a few hours," replied Bristow. "They think they've found some of the Fiora Collection and would like me to examine the stones."

"I hope to goodness they're right," Mannering said fervently.

Bristow had spent months, spread over several years, searching for a collection of rubies and emeralds stolen from a Mayfair house some seven years ago, and he was as eager as ever to see them recovered. Mannering had four appointments in the office that afternoon and so would be in all the time; Bristow being out would cause no problems.

He, Mannering, went out to a small club-restaurant for lunch, walking to St. James's Street, his stride long and brisk.

Every time he saw a long-haired youth, he thought of Forrester; and every time he saw a girl in a mini-skirt he thought of Julie. He was reminded of them again when he found himself sitting across the long table from Paul Bayonard, who owned several small Mayfair art galleries and had an interest in some provincial ones in or near big cities. The service, by a middle-aged woman dressed in a black dress adorned with an old-fashioned lace cap and apron, was very good; the English fare even better.

Mannering had steak, kidney and oyster pie; Bayonard, a trout with sliced almonds.

"Paul," Mannering asked, "have you ever heard of a young and struggling artist named Forrester?"

"Forrester, Forrester," echoed Bayonard. "The name rings a bell. What does he do?"

"He is a self-styled genius," declared Mannering.

"What, another?" Bayonard raised his eyebrows. "Don't say he fooled you, John."

"I haven't seen his work yet," Mannering said. "He has a very pretty girl-friend, named Julie, who —"

"Oh, *now* I remember!" Bayonard's eyes lit up. "He's the chap who punched Parsons on the nose — presumably for making improper proposals." Bayonard leaned forward to inspect. "Your nose seems all right, I must say."

"And will remain so! What does Forrester do?"

"He used to be good at fakes — or copies, but he won't do them any more, his artistic soul revolted. He concentrates on his form of sex art in great variety but never in quality. He must have been refused by more galleries than any other artist under fifty, and turned down with damning regularity. How did you come to meet him?"

Mannering began to dissemble and was helped when a newcomer sat down next to him and another by Bayonard. The first was a provincial antique dealer who had obviously come deliberately to sit next to Mannering, who was among London's top twelve dealers — and so judges — in the world. The other owned a large Chelsea art gallery not far from the Town Hall. The conversation became general until, when they were drinking coffee, Bayonard asked the other picture expert:

"John says he's interested in Tom Forrester, Stephen."

Stephen, young, long-faced, nearly bald, with well-cut clothes and beautifully kept hands, raised artificial-looking dark eyebrows.

"Don't be," he advised.

"Why not?"

"He is the inevitable second-rater who thinks he is a genius."

"Sure?"

"Yes. Touch him, and you'll burn your fingers." Then Stephen grinned, and asked teasingly: "Who approached you — Forrester or his Julie?"

"Both together," answered Mannering.

"No wonder you're interested! But the answer is still 'don't'. Have you told him about how he broke Parsons' nose?" Stephen asked, eagerly.

"So it's broken now, is it?"

"A hair fracture, I'm told, and that won't do any harm

if it teaches Parsons to keep his paws off the girls. Funny thing," he went on, "but some of these young people who live together in trial marriages, as one might say, are more fiercely protective of their mates than a lot of staid married couples. There must be a moral for the times in that."

A general laugh rewarded this sally.

Mannering left soon afterwards, reaching Quinns with only five minutes to go before his first appointment. Two dealers and two old customers came in quick succession, and it was nearly five o'clock before he had finished and could relax. Bristow had not yet returned but it proved to have been a quiet day in the shop; one of those days when he felt he could safely leave early with Armitage and Rupert Smith in charge. But he had hardly opened the door than Rupert called out :

"Telephone for you, sir ! A lady."

There was an instrument by the door, which closed as Mannering placed the receiver to his ear and announced :

"John Mannering."

"Mr. Mannering," a girl said. "Tom's tried to kill himself. Please come and help him — *please*." Before Mannering had gone much further than realise that it was Julie, talking of Forrester, she went on as if in despair : "It's 17 Riston Street, Fulham. Oh, please come !"

3

Noose and Knot

RISTON STREET, FULHAM, WAS not far from Wandsworth
Bridge, in an area which all new and tall buildings had
by-passed. It was still much as it had been half-a-century
before. The houses were in short, narrow terraces. Each
house was two storeys high and each had a slate roof, but
there much of the similarity ended. Some had brick walls
in front of tiny gardens or yards which saved the front
windows from abutting the street. Some were near derelict;
others shone in new high gloss paint, and while most were
white with a red motif of bricks round the doors and windows, some were blue or green or yellow. One, at a corner
was vividly purple.

Number 17 was drab; unpainted; unadorned.

A few small cars were parked on either side of the street
but there was plenty of room for Mannering to park. He
had come in a Morris station wagon, used for Quinns as
a delivery van, not in his own Allard; yet even the wagon
was resplendent here and a few people, already home from
work, glanced at it and at him with curiosity reserved for
the unfamiliar. Mannering was not only handsome but
taller than most, and his Savile Row tailor did full justice
to his broad figure.

He stepped into the narrow porch of Number 17, half-
turned, and banged his elbow. As he rubbed it, he caught
his knuckles on the rough brick surface of the porch, so
little room was there. Then he espied two bell pushes, one

white, one black, on the wooden door frame, and above the
top one was a typewritten name : *Forrester.*

So Forrester had taken over Julie's flat !

Careful not to graze his fingers again, he pressed the
bell. There was no immediate response, so he rang for a
second time. Soon he heard hurried footsteps which grew
louder as someone came running down the stairs. He
backed a little as the door opened, and Julie stood there.

She was dressed exactly as she had been at the shop, but
her eyes were huge and bright and her face alive with
alarm — and suddenly with enormous relief.

"Oh, thank you, thank you !" she gasped. "Please come
in."

The passage was narrow and, when the door was closed,
very gloomy. A flight of steps, narrow wooden stairs led
upwards; a narrow passage ran alongside these. There were
four closed doors, but as they reached the foot of the stairs
one at the end of the passage opened a crack and a very
old man appeared. He stood, watching from eyes deep in
dark sockets.

"I'll go first," Julie volunteered, and ran nimbly up the
stairs; the mini-skirt revealed again how nice her legs were,
slender yet well-shaped. At the head of the stairs was a
small, square landing, with three doors leading off; the
only light came from two of the doors, which stood open.
One, on the left, was wider open than the others, but as
Mannering passed one, he saw a rope — a noose — hanging from the ceiling; and beneath it a chair, fallen on its
side.

"*Here,*" Julie breathed from the door on the left, and
he followed her in.

Until this moment he had wondered if this were some
kind of trick, or hoax; from the very beginning, it had been
so strange. But there was no hoax about the man who lay
on the large divan bed. He was unconscious. He lay on his
back, wearing jeans, moccasin shoes and an open-necked
shirt. The rope marks at his neck, beneath the chin, were
quite unmistakable. The aquiline appearance was much

more noticeable than at the shop, his pointed chin and his sharp nose seemed to jut out from the sunken cheeks and the high forehead.

It was like looking at the embalmed figure of a man, for Forrester was so alabaster white.

"He can't be asleep." Mannering took the long, thin hand and searched with his forefinger for the pulse.

"He — he banged his head when I — when I got him down," Julie confessed in a husky voice. "I managed to loosen the rope."

Her voice trailed off and she swayed away from Mannering. As he grabbed her, taking her weight, her knees sagged and she would have fallen but for him. He lifted her, looked around, saw only wooden, upright chairs, and placed her on the divan next to Forrester. She wasn't fully unconscious and kept trying to open her eyes, but he put a bright red cushion under her head, and said quietly :

"Keep still, Julie. You'll both be all right." He sat on a corner of the divan, on a bright green folk-weave bed-spread, and took a brandy flask from his hip pocket. On a bedside table was a tea tray, in one saucer a spoon, so he poured brandy into the spoon and then, manoeuvring care-fully, eased her up with one arm and put the spoon close to her lips. "Sip this slowly," he ordered, and she opened her mouth slightly but not her eyes. Her lips hardly moved but she did swallow; he noticed the faint movements at her throat. He gave her two more spoonsful, and when she had got these down she shook her head as if to say 'enough'.

Mannering stood up, stretched, replaced the cap and put the flask back in his pocket, then rounded the divan and checked Forrester's pulse again. It was steady enough but seemed very faint. He made a closer inspection of the rope marks, and detected an odour of antiseptic; so Julie had bathed them.

She was proving a remarkable young woman.

She muttered : "How — how is he?"

"I think he's all right," answered Mannering. "How long has he been unconscious?"

"He was only just conscious when I got him down, and
— well, I gave him a sleeping tablet."

"It must have been some tablet to put him out like that,"
Mannering said lightly, and when she began to sit up, as
if to talk, he leaned across and pressed her shoulders firmly.
"Stay there for a while and take it easy," he ordered. "I'll
make some tea or coffee.

She nodded, fair hair vivid against the crimson cushion.

He glanced out of the window, which overlooked the
street, where more cars were being parked as the residents
came home, then went to the door, turned, and looked into
the room. The first impression had been a vague one, of
colours and brightness, and this remained, except that there
was more planning about the colouring than he had
thought, on chairs and wall, on bed and old furniture obviously bought at second, third or fourth hand, the few
vases including a beautiful white swan had a careless look
which was in fact carefully arranged. Only someone with
an artist's eye could possibly have done this.

Forrester? Or Julie?

There were unframed paintings on the wall, some ab-
stract, one of this street which when he examined it closely
was almost a daub; but when he stood back it fell into
perspective, and the effect was startlingly good.

He turned to the square landing.

One room, where the noose dangled, was a bathroom.
This held a big old-fashioned claw-footed bath painted
with nudes both male and female, against a misty back-
ground which might have been an ocean or might be
meant as sky. On the high gloss of the wall paint there was
a medley of female bosoms, without heads, without bodies,
just the breasts in great variety. On one wall, where the
light of the window fell, the effect was quite startling, for
the skin and the colouring of the nipples seemed so real.

Only the lavatory seat was unadorned. The pedestal
itself was painted vivid red, with white and black spots.

Mannering looked upwards, and had his biggest shock
yet. For the noose dropped from a hole in the ceiling

which had an ethereal light, while the ceiling itself was covered with pictures of bodies, chubby children with golden curls, skeletal children like those from Africa's famine-torn lands. Black, white and yellow, babies of every imaginable race and shade and size, all having one thing in common.

Every mouth was open; seeking food.

Every mouth was turned towards the bosoms on the walls.

Mannering thought : Is he a fetishist? Is he sex-mad?

He made himself look up into the attic, his eyes now so accustomed to the pale light that he could see that the other end of the rope was tied to a beam. He was tempted to climb up; by stepping on to the W.C. pedestal it would be easy enough. But he had already been here for several minutes, so he went into the other room, opposite the head of the stairs — and again was startled.

In front of the small window was a sink, a draining board, and next to this a small gas oven. Against one wall, a table and two wooden chairs, painted yellow. But every square inch of the other two walls was covered with paintings; heads, shoulders, hands, feet, knees, elbows and wrists — every part of the human body was depicted there, none drawn or painted with great precision, each at first having a daubed-on look. But each had vividness; and each became life-like, growing on one, as it were.

Mannering put on a kettle, igniting the gas from a flintlighter, then went back to the front room.

Julie, still on her back, seemed to be dozing; and Forrester was exactly as he had left him. He drew a folkweave blanket, folded at the foot of the divan, up to Julie's shoulders, and she didn't stir, so he returned to the kitchen, turned the gas low, and went back to the bathroom. The noose hung about a yard beneath the hatch, and a wooden chair lay on its side by the wall. He placed one hand just above the noose and put one foot on the pedestal and drew himself up until his head and shoulders were inside the attic and he was able to haul himself higher.

The light came from a square window in the roof, so that the roof seemed and, in a way, was open to the sky. A dormer window had been built near this and an easel stood in position to catch this north light. There was just room in front of the easel for a man of medium height to stand. Everywhere else, anyone would have to stand hunched, for the attic beams were low.

And each was adorned, much as the kitchen and the bathroom, but here were faces of men and women, boys and girls, faces of every shape and size and colour and, even more impressive, of expression. And there were paintings of nudes, male and female locked together in strange postures; much more here that could be called 'sex art'; yet none was beastly.

The unframed pictures, some on hardboard, some on canvas or on paper, took up every spare inch of space. By the side of the easel were some shelves, with paints and rags and bottles of turpentine, powder, brushes; everything was orderly and at hand.

And on the easel was a painting of him, John Mannering.

It was small and done in oils, and the paint was far from dry. There was no doubt at all that he was the subject; no doubt about the face of the devil cunningly superimposed; there were even small, pointed horns, while the turn of his lips was satyrish. It was as if Forrester had drawn the face and then painted over it, to get the effect of showing the real man — the devil! — behind the handsome surface.

Slowly, Mannering moved so that he could see it from every angle.

He thought, as he often thought since Forrester had visited him, of Lorna, his wife. She was one of the best and most renowned portrait painters in England, and he wondered what she would think of this.

He studied the faces more closely, and came upon a likeness of Bayonard, with an 'inner face' of self-indulgence and smugness; near this, one of Stephen who had been at the club for lunch. Gradually, Mannering realised that many of the likenesses — even on the couples who were interlocked — were of the owners and managers of picture galleries, of contemporary artists, of curators and directors of big art galleries like the Royal Academy and the Tate. It was as if Forrester had a private hate for all of these and showed them, here, in the merciless light in which he saw them.

Mannering went to the dormer window.

It overlooked acre upon acre of grey slate roofs and red chimney pots and brick or cemented chimney stacks; an unending vista startlingly vivid in the late afternoon sunlight. Even close to he could not see into the gardens or below the eaves and guttering.

At last, he went down exactly the way he had come up. The kettle was singing. A brown earthenware tea pot stood upside down on the draining board, cups and saucers with it. A tea-caddy contained loose tea. He made a pot, found another cheap metal tray, loaded it and took it into the front room, where there was milk in a jug on the other tray.

Julie was awake, looking at him. Her eyes were shadowed, but there was more colour in her cheeks.

"Better?" he asked.

"Yes, thank you. Much."

"Feel like some tea?"

"I'd love a cup."

"Good," he said, and glanced at Forrester as she hitched herself up on the divan. "Just what happened, Julie?"

She said slowly : "We had a quarrel after we left you, and I didn't come straight home. When I got back, he —" she shivered, and the colour faded. "I saw him — hanging."

"And got him down," Mannering remarked, wryly. "What a terrible task that must have been."

"Yes. He — he fell and bumped his head."

"I saw the bruise."

"I managed to get him to bed," she went on, "and — and when he began to come round I asked him what had happened, and he said he didn't know, didn't see anyone.

He began to get excited, so I made him take the tablet. He thought it was an aspirin." She was watching Mannering all the time. "Everything was — horrible."

He could envisage the whole scene; picture her getting the knife, loosening the rope, trying to save Forrester from falling. She must have been exhausted when she had finished. He poured out tea in an effort to bring a touch of normality, and she sat up straight and took a cup.

"Sugar?"

"No, thank you." She sipped. "I rushed out to telephone as soon as he'd gone to sleep. I've a room in a house across the street and the people there let me use their telephone — I baby-sit for them sometimes, when they're both out at work. So I have a key."

"Did she hear you telephone me?" asked Mannering.

"No, no one did. The house was empty."

"Julie," began Mannering gently. "Why did you call me, of all people?"

She sipped her tea again but didn't answer at once. He sat on the bottom corner of the bed, also drinking tea. Julie's hair was dishevelled, and looked like spun gold against a simulated bed panel painted on the wall, a deep purple which seemed designed to show her hair to best advantage.

"There — there just wasn't anyone else," she said at last. "Besides —" She hesitated, but Mannering did not try to hurry her, and slowly she went on : "All the way home I could think only of one thing : how I could persuade you to come here." When he stayed silent, she continued with considered frankness : "I wanted you here desperately. I believed you were simpatico."

"With Tom or with you?" asked Mannering.

"With art," she answered simply. "I didn't think you would allow personal feelings to get in the way of art."

With a faint smile, he said : "I try not to."

"I can tell you do. I —" she stretched out her left hand, small, white, unadorned without even a ring of pretence, and said pleadingly : "You would help if you thought Tom worthwhile, wouldn't you?"

"Yes," answered Mannering. "I'd try."

"Despite his — his arrogance?"

"Yes," he repeated simply.

She eyed him searchingly. He had no idea what was passing through her mind but was quite sure she was searching for words to express exactly what she felt. And they came slowly, while her eyes were glowing, appealing, as if she were begging him to tell the truth.

"And not — not because of me?" she pleaded. "Not because you either feel sorry for me, or think that if you play your cards right you will persuade me to go to bed with you. It would be because — because you believe in art, wouldn't it?"

Now her gaze was both direct and challenging, as if she were daring him to lie to her : as if she wanted to lay bare his mind so that she could be sure that whatever answer he gave was the truth.

4

Art for Art's Sake

IT SEEMED A LONG time before Mannering answered, and
when he did it was in a matter-of-fact voice carrying just
a hint of reproof. He felt at once deeply compassionate
towards her and at the same time a little angry. He finished
his tea, put the cup down and remarked :

"Tom thinks his painting is irresistibly good, doesn't
he?"

"Yes, he does."

"And you think your body is irresistible, too, don't
you?"

She winced; drew back; and began to lose her colour.
It was the last response that she had expected, so she
wasn't in any way prepared for it. Mannering watched her
very closely, thinking how beautiful she was, and how
desirable any man who allowed his feelings to roam would
find her.

"I didn't — I didn't think of it that way," she said at
last.

"Have you found men so predatory?" he asked.

"Pred — oh, yes." She paused, caught her breath and
went on : "Yes. Most of them. They seem to think that
because we younger people want a permissive society,
because we won't accept a lot of the conventions, that
we're all promiscuous, that — well, one pair of arms is like
another."

"Don Quixote," Mannering murmured.

"Dulcinea," she said huskily. "I — I'm sorry."

"I think I ought to apologise for the kind of men you've met," Mannering responded gently.

"It's not that!" she exclaimed, suddenly angry. "It's not just some kind of men. I have to go and ask them for something and it's like a reflex action for them to ask me what I'm going to pay with. You — *you* seem to be the exception."

Mannering made no response.

"Mr. Mannering," she said, "will you help Tom?"

"If he'll let me," Mannering replied.

"What do you mean by that?"

"If he'll accept whatever I'm able to suggest," Mannering answered, leaning forward and taking her free hand in both of his. "Julie, you know as well as I do that it would be folly for anyone simply to offer to support him until he can support himself. That could break any real spirit he has left." When she didn't answer, he went on : "You do realise that some way has to be found for him to help himself, don't you?"

"I suppose so," Julie sighed. "What — what do you think you could do?"

"Before I can give any opinion I need to talk to him again, and also a chance to look at his work more closely, and I would like my wife to see his paintings. Do you know who she is?"

"Yes," Julie replied. "She paints portraits as Lorna Fauntley."

"That's right."

"She is very good," Julie declared. "If —" she broke off.

"If traditional," Mannering finished for her.

"I really didn't mean to be rude," Julie said, flushing a little. "I'm so tired, absolutely worn out and — and living with Tom is like living next to a volcano. He's desperate, Mr. Mannering. It doesn't matter what he tries to do, it turns sour on him. And he feel's he's let me down. At first he fought against letting me help but eventually he had to, or else starve, so he gave way. I came home one day after going to a gallery where a man offered to buy some of Tom's pictures if I would sleep with him, and I told Tom. I shouldn't have, but I was so upset. He went straight off and attacked the man, and ever since then he's been much more difficult, sometimes almost uncontrollable, and terribly moody. I've been afraid he might kill himself, but this is the first time he's tried." She paused, and he squeezed her hand; and then she went on: "If I'd been twenty minutes — ten minutes later, he would probably have died."

"Yes," Mannering said. "You certainly saved his life."

"After driving him to attempt suicide!"

"Nonsense! Circumstances and my attitude this afternoon did that." Mannering gave her hand a final squeeze and let it go. "What do you do, to keep things going, Julie?"

"Type," she answered.

"Just type?"

"Yes — manuscripts for authors, memos, reports, letters — any kind of typing. I built up a connection years ago, that's how I've always earned my living. I've a little room across the street, and pay for it partly by baby-sitting, as I told you. It's better than working here. I don't interrupt Tom and he does not interrupt me."

"And Tom?"

"He paints," she replied heavily.

"Does he ever sell *anything*?"

"Not since he stopped painting copies and what he calls pretty picture postcard scenes. He has to paint as he *sees* things, creatively, and even then —" once Julie broke off, as if reluctant to finish what she had started to say.

"Please go on," he urged her.

"He won't sell for nothing or next to nothing! If he'd accept two or three guineas for a picture he would make a few sales, but his lowest price is ten guineas and that's low enough." She looked at Mannering defiantly. "It may sound arrogant but he is right in one way. He really *is*."

"Yes," Mannering said. "Or he would be if he could

keep the wolf from the door. What made him come to see me, do you know?"

"There was an article about you in *The Antiquarian Dealer*," she answered. "It said you believed that artists should have patrons, as in the olden day way, that if a man was really potentially good he needed to be able to concentrate on his work, not just on finding food and drink. You *did* say that, didn't you?" She caught her breath, as if fearful that he would deny it.

"And believe it," Mannering assured her. "The trouble is to decide whom to back, Julie. There are a hundred artists who think they deserve it to every one who really does." He stood up and went to the window, hearing a car pull up outside; it was a small one on the far side of the road. A tall, fair-haired young woman got out, carrying a baby, and a good-looking, easy-moving man appeared on the other side and led the way to a house which was painted blue and had *No. 20* painted in white on the blue above the porch. "I went up into the attic, and spent a little time in the kitchen and the bathroom," he went on. "Are all the paintings Tom's?"

"Yes. They *are* good, aren't they?" Again, her heart seemed to be in her mouth.

"I like the look of a lot of them," Mannering told her, turning to face her. "How does he offer them?"

"Well, how *can* he? He takes them round in portfolios or in suit-cases, and shows them to the dealers." When Mannering didn't respond, she went on: "How else *can* he offer them?"

"I'm nearly sure that isn't the way," Mannering replied.

"Then what *is*, for goodness sake?"

"Give me a little time to think," Mannering begged.

"Oh, I will!" There was fresh brightness in her eyes, eagerness and hope. "You are really serious, aren't you?"

"Yes," Mannering said. "I'm really serious."

"So you *do* believe in art for art's sake!" she cried.

"I'm not so sure about that," Mannering replied. "I believe that there is a commercial future in these paintings, and if there weren't I wouldn't be so inclined to help." He laughed at the expression on her face. "Don't be too disappointed, Julie! History's made it clear that the greater the art the greater the price that should be paid for it! There *is* a direct relation between quality and fees even today, you know."

"I suppose there is," Julie said, but she did not sound convinced. "I can't thank you enough for — for saying you'd try." She pushed the folk-weave blanket off her and began to get off the bed. "What do you think I ought to do with Tom, now?"

"How long do you think he'll sleep?"

"Four or five more hours, at least," she said, and looked at a tiny travelling clock on the mantelpiece. "Goodness! It's half-past six!"

"And so he'll sleep until midnight," Mannering said. "No need to worry about him."

"It isn't that," she cried. "I should have been with the Pagets, I'm always there at six o'clock to help with the baby. I must fly."

"Julie!" Mannering said sharply. "You're not well enough to rush about."

"But I must! It's — it's my job, it's why I get the room free for working. I must —"

She spun round, staggered, and obviously turned dizzy. She pushed a hand against the door to steady herself but it closed under her weight and she fell against it. He reached her just in time to save her from falling, and she stood shivering with his arm round her shoulders.

"Julie," he said gently. "You're suffering from shock, and you must have some rest." He helped her back to bed, and she made no protest, even when he pulled the blanket up over her again. "I'll go across and explain to the Pagets," he promised. "Are they close friends?"

"Not — not really friends, they —" she shot out an arm. "You won't tell them what Tom did, will you? *Please.*"

"I shall not. Do you want them to come over?"

"I'd rather just rest, please." She was shivering, and he

looked round for another cover and found only a lamb's
wool top-coat, which he spread over her.

"That's more like it! May I borrow your key?"

"Why — oh, yes, do. It's in my bag."

Her bag was a felt one with some velvet patterns em-
bossed on it, and the keys were on the top of a jumble of
cosmetics, letters, matches, handkerchiefs and tickets. He
took the keys and turned to her.

"Do the Pagets live at Number 20?"

"Yes. How did you know?"

"They've only just got home," Mannering tried to reassure her. "I won't be long."

By the time he reached the front door he was aware of
the old grey-haired man peering from a partly open door,
and of a curious sense of unreality. When he closed the
front door it was like turning his back on a dream. But
this was no dream, and it could have been stark tragedy.
A youth on a motor-cycle passed slowly, an ancient car
swung into the nearer end of the road; and he waited for
this to pass before crossing. There was much less room to
park, now, although still a few vacant spaces. The car
outside Number 20 was a dark green M.G., which suggested
that the Pagets were reasonably successful. A child's toy
was on the passenger seat next to the driver, other baby
oddments on the back seat. He opened the blue-painted
gate and pressed a brass surrounded bell-push centred on
the front door which was painted the same colour.

Footsteps sounded almost at once, and as the door opened
the man whom Mannering had seen getting out of the car
appeared. He was of medium height, had an athletic looking figure and wore a suit not unlike the Edwardian elegance of the two assistants at Quinns. He was dark-haired
and dark-jowled, obviously having to shave twice a day.
Yet his cheeks, where there was no incipient stubble, were
apple-red, his face was rather broad-featured, his nose
rather short and slightly tip-tilted; and he had a big cleft
in his chin.

"Good evening." He looked puzzled.

"Good evening," said Mannering. "Are you Mr. Paget?"

"Clive Paget, yes," the other answered. "And you? —"

"My name is Mannering, John Mannering. I've just come from Julie and Tom Forrester," Mannering said. "I wonder if you can spare me a few minutes."

"Of course," Clive Paget said. "Come in." As he backed into the hall and stood close to the wall, he called out: "It's someone from Tom and Julie, love."

At the door at the end of the passage identical in lay-out to the house across the street, was the fair-haired young woman, who had the baby in her arms. It was almost as if there had been some strange metamorphosis and the old man had changed into the attractive girl. The door closed slowly and the blonde's face was the last thing he saw.

"Let's go in here," Paget said, and opened the door of a room opposite the stairs. It was small but surprisingly bright, with one large window overlooking the back of the house. Slantwise across the window was a typist's desk with a large typewriter on it, some papers and odds and ends. Against one wall stood a filing cabinet, against the third, a trestle table. The room was very orderly, and gave an impression of precise organisation. "Julie works in here." Paget went on. "We couldn't understand why she wasn't here when we got back, she's usually so dependable." Then, belatedly, an expression of concern crossed his face and his dark, brown eyes glowed as if with anxiety. "But what's wrong? Is she all right?" He gripped Mannering's forearm.

"Forrester had a bit of trouble climbing down from the attic," Mannering said, "and Julie had her work cut out to get him to bed and manage first aid."

Paget looked alarmed.

"Does she need help? Shall I go across? Or Doris —"

"They're both fine now," Mannering assured him. "I arrived just after the accident and was able to help a bit. Tom is resting, and I persuaded Julie not to come across to you."

"Quite right, too," approved Paget. "Well, I'm glad it's no worse. She's such a worker! Sometimes I feel sorry — but that's neither here nor there! Er —" Paget pursed his lips, frowned and then relaxed and asked: "May I ask what took you there, Mr. Mannering?"

"I'd come to see his pictures," Mannering answered.

"Oh, I *see*! Julie never stops trying! Did you — er — form any conclusion?"

"There was a lot of confusion and I didn't get a good look," Mannering replied. "I'll have to come again."

"Confusion? Oh, about the accident — of course! Yes, there would be. Did you have time to have a glance into the bathroom for instance?"

"A very quick one, yes."

He was keenly aware of the brightness of Paget's dark eyes, of an expression which was both cautious and bold at the same time. Obviously some remark was on the tip of Paget's tongue, but he wasn't sure whether he ought to make it. Then he made up his mind and his expression was a cross between a smile and a leer. He thrust his face a little closer to Mannering's.

"He's a bit of a queer, isn't he? Tom, I mean. A bit obscene, if you know what I mean. All those bosoms in the bathroom! He's obsessed with sex, not much doubt about that, is there?"

"He's preoccupied with some aspects of it, anyhow," Mannering conceded.

"That's one way of putting it! Well, I hope he makes a go of it if only for Julie's sake. She really is a sweetie. She *is* all right, isn't she?"

"Completely all right," Mannering assured him. "She wanted to come over as usual and I persuaded her that it would be best for them both if they relaxed completely and had an early night."

"Jolly good idea," approved Paget. "And if you're going back over there tell her not to worry but call on us if she needs anything. *We*," he went on, stressing the plural pronoun, "are very fond of Julie."

"She is certainly most charming," Mannering said.

"Charming's the word! She —" Paget broke off again, and turned to the door. "Tell her we hope Tom soon gets over the accident," he repeated, and led the way into the narrow hall. "Er — do you think the paintings *are* any good?"

Mannering dissembled. "The real question is whether he has a future, and that's hard to judge."

Paget opened the street door and ushered him out with many 'Goodbyes'. Mannering had a feeling of unease, not liking the man yet suspicious even of his own first reactions, as he crossed the street. Two boys came tearing along on roller skates and he froze. They skimmed round him, one giving a cheeky grin. He let himself into the house, smiling, and was startled to find the wizened, grey-haired man already at the foot of the stairs. He was very round-shouldered and frail looking, but turned round with surprising speed as Mannering stepped inside. In a wheezy, querulous voice, he asked :

"Is everything all right with them hippies upstairs," he wanted to know. "Tell me now. Is it?"

"As far as I know everything's fine," Mannering assured him. "What makes you think it might not be?"

"I heard a hell of a thump," the old man wheezed. "Felt as if the whole house was falling down, it did. Frightened the wits out of me." He waited for Mannering to reach him but did not budge from the spot and so barred Mannering's way. "I don't want no one murdered in my house, mister."

Mannering asked sharply: "What do you mean by murder?"

"Those hippies are always murdering one another, like they did in Californy," the old man charged. "I don't want none of that here in my house. You just tell them so, mister."

"Aren't they good tenants?" asked Mannering sharply.

"Oh, they pay their rent regular," the other conceded. "But I'm not so sure I hold with all those pictures they paint, it doesn't seem decent to me. And the way they quarrel sometimes, it's something awful. Just so that they don't start murdering each other that's all I care. You tell them."

He glared demandingly at Mannering for several seconds, then turned and shuffled along the passage. Mannering felt sure that he could hear the old bones creaking.

5

The Noose Again

MANNERING WAS SMILING FAINTLY to himself, yet was half-frowning, too. It was one thing to be amused by the old man's obvious conviction that all hippies were potential murderers, but his complaint about the quarrels wasn't funny. Why should he lie? And if he told the truth, how often and how violent were the quarrels?

Mannering went back to the front room.

Julie was on her side, knees drawn up, looking towards him. Her face had an elfin look, but her eyes were heavy and shadowed.

"How are you?" Mannering asked.

"I've a terrible headache," she answered. "I got out of bed just now and took some aspirins, so I'll be all right soon. What did Mrs. Paget say?"

"I told them Tom had fallen down from the attic," Mannering answered, "and that you both needed an early night. They promised not to bother you but said you're to go to them if you need help."

"And I will," Julie promised. "They're really very nice."

"Sure you won't mind being left alone here?"

"Of course not!" she rallied to a scornful smile. "I'm often alone all night." She stretched out a hand pleadingly. "You *will* help Tom, won't you?"

"If he'll help himself, yes," Mannering promised. "Now, I'm off!" He stepped to the door, and opened it wider, then on impulse looked down at her and asked: "Do you mind if I go up into the attic?"

"Go where you like," she said, without hesitation.

"I won't disturb you again," Mannering said. "But I'll look round about eleven o'clock."

"Oh, you needn't —" she began, but he went out and closed the door firmly.

There was no sound in the house and only a few street noises, while not far off a baby was crying; it couldn't be the Paget's could it? He stepped into the bathroom and the crying sounded louder; the crying baby was in one of the nearby houses. He looked up at the hole in the ceiling, and was startled when he saw that the noose was missing. Julie must have taken it down or pushed it up into the attic. It made little difference, he could get a grip on the sides of the hole, and haul himself up. It was harder than he had expected, and he strained his muscles, staring up to the softer light of the attic. At last his head and shoulders were above the level of the attic floor.

God!

A man crouched on one side, the rope in his hands, the noose raised. And before he could let go and drop to the floor, it dropped about his neck.

And it tightened.

In that awful moment he did not know what to do, although thoughts flashed through his mind with panic swiftness. If he let go his full weight would drop on to the rope and on to his neck, he could easily break his neck. He must not let go. He moved his legs, groping desperately for the bath or the pedestal, touched the bath which gave out a hollow boom, took a little of his weight on his left foot, and on the instant felt searing pain in the fingers of his left hand. *A man was stamping on them.* He let go, hanging on now by one hand, groping for a better hold with his feet and groping with his free hand for the rope above the noose.

The man up there trod on his right hand.

If he let go, the jolt on his neck would be so severe that it might break.

He made a great effort and got both feet on the bath

and gripped the rope so that the whole of his weight was off his neck and the noose for a split-second; and in that split-second he swept his left hand into the attic, felt and grabbed the man's ankles, and pulled savagely.

The man crashed down, inside the attic, at the very moment when Mannering's feet slipped off the edge of the bath. In a despairing grab he clutched the edge of the hole, getting grip enough to break his fall.

Now, he had only one hope: to pull himself up into the attic while the man was off his balance.

His neck felt as if it were being stretched, his eyes burned and there was great pressure against them. His tongue hurt, his jaws ached, his shoulders felt as if he were bearing a ton weight. He knew all of these things as he drew a deep breath, tensed the muscles of his arms and shoulders, and hauled himself up.

And as he went into the attic, Julie cried out, a kind of muted scream:

"Oh, no, no, no!"

Mannering got a knee over the side, saw an upright beam and managed to grip it, felt sharp pain as a splinter went into the ball of a middle finger, then pulled himself into the attic, first on his knees, then on his feet, crouching; for the beams and the roof were low.

"What's happening? What's happening?" Julie's voice, still sounding far away, was filled as if with terror.

The man was at the skylight, pushing at it, Mannering could just make out the stocking-mask over his face, the black jacket, the jeans. Rafters between them slowed Mannering down. The man was half-turned towards him, working desperately at a catch on the window. He was within a hand's reach of the bottles, grabbed one and hurled it at Mannering, who dodged and banged his head on a beam hard enough to make him gasp. The bottle dropped but did not break. Mannering caught a glimpse of Julie's upturned face and burning eyes as he straddled a rafter.

The rooflight opened. The man pushed harder and it

lodged into an upright position. The man clutched the edges and hauled himself through. He had on a pair of pale brown suede ankle shoes, that was all Mannering could see as he drew himself out to the roof.

"*Are you all right?*" Julie screamed.

Mannering called in a voice which reverberated among the rafters and the pictures : "Yes, don't worry." He hoisted himself through the rooflight in one swift movement : went out of the attic and on to the slate roof.

And with the movement, there was a metamorphosis; it was as if the years rolled away and as he stood here, balanced precariously against a chimney stack and the slates, he was the other self that he had been long, long ago.

He was the Baron.

He was the man of his youth, daring, dazzling; taking risks which would have cowed most men; sometimes giving chase to criminals, as he was now, sometimes on the run from the police who had often been close on his heels. Then he had been jewel-thief extraordinary, cracksman, and also a kind of Robin Hood, robbing the rich to help the poor. Further back, long years further back, he had been a thief both for the thrill and for the gain, robbing only the wealthy and yet on the wrong side of the law and for a few brief years, making his living from his daring thefts.

It was like a vivid series of flashbacks. The excitement and the danger had brought them to him; if he slipped he would roll down the roof and crash, breaking bones even if he did not kill himself.

All these flashes took only swift moments of time; and while the cloak of the past spread over him, he scanned the roof — and caught sight of the man who had so nearly hanged him. The man was peering behind a chimney stack amid that forest of small red chimneys, two or three sending smoke drifting lazily towards the cloudless sky. The roofs of this row of houses were continuous, and there was a flat ridge running across the top, broken by chimney stacks each of which obviously served two houses. He was breathing easily now and felt completely poised and confident, in spite of soreness of his fingers, grazed where the man had stamped on them. He walked along one section of the ledge to the next chimney stack, actually pulling the splinter out of his finger. He reached the stack and peered round, then saw something dark hurtling towards him, twisting and turning.

It was a slate off the roof. If it struck him, it could lay his cheek open to the bone.

He ducked.

It passed a few inches above his head, and crashed on to the roof behind him. He made a swift movement towards the next chimney stack but when he was halfway between the two, another slate came skimming through the air, about chin high. He could not go either right or left, all he could do was bend his knees and crouch down.

The slate missed; he did not know by how much.

He heard it crash with deafening noise, and almost immediately heard someone shouting down in the street.

"Look out!"

"Careful!"

A woman screamed: "Mind, Georgey!"

Another slate came hurtling while others, loosened, began to slither down.

Mannering, crouching, reached the next chimney stack, heart in mouth. No more slates were in the air, but how could he tell when another might come? There were more cries from below but nothing to suggest that anyone had been hurt. It was surprising how clearly the voices sounded.

"There's someone up there."

"Bloody lunatic."

"We ought to send for the police."

"That's right — police!"

Mannering held his breath as he ventured on the ledge towards the next stack, and as he did so, caught a glimpse of the stockinged face. His assailant was several houses along, lowering himself over the edge to a back-garden.

So there would be no more danger from slates, and Mannering quickened his pace, watching the other all the time.

The head disappeared, but he was still holding on to the guttering by his hands. Mannering tried to quicken his pace, but a slate moved under his feet, slowed him down. Turning his back on the spot where the man had disappeared, he spread-eagled himself face downwards, and, clutching the rough edges of the slates, lowered himself until his feet lodged against the guttering. This was the spot where the man had gone over, if there were a chance to catch him it was by dropping over the edge.

A woman shouted from the back-garden.

A child cried out: "Look, Mummy!"

Then the guttering gave way under Mannering's weight, and he went hurtling down.

For the first moment, he thought he would go all the way to the ground, and could not avoid injury, but suddenly his feet jolted against a hard, unyielding drain pipe and his ankles and knees were shot with pain. Next moment he was on his hands and knees on top of a pebbly roof, the blood rushing to his head.

The child was screaming: "Mummy, Mummy!"

A woman shouted: "Benny! Benny, come here!"

Mannering got unsteadily to his knees, and it placed him so that he could see into the back-garden. The fugitive was opening a small gate which led into an alleyway between two rows of garden walls. A child of four or five years was standing and shouting, red apple of a face glistening. A woman in her thirties was running towards him, and as the gate slammed she snatched him to her.

"It's all right, Benny, it's all right!" she gasped, as footsteps sounded in the alley.

Mannering eased his position until he was sitting down, and then began to feel his knees, hands and elbows gingerly. There was a graze on the ball of his left thumb, his fingers were sore and his knees were tender, and one of his ankles was painful, but he did not think any bones were broken. The sound of footsteps faded, and he knew that his assailant had escaped.

But someone might have stopped him at the end of the alley.

He peered along, seeing no one and no sign of movement until suddenly the small boy pointed and said again:

"Look, Mummy!"

The woman stared up, aghast.

"I'm really not a thief," Mannering assured her, in his most pleasant voice. "I was chasing a bad man. Sorry if I scared you." He waited for a few moments, seeing suspicion and doubt chase each other in the woman's eyes, and curiosity shine in the child's. The woman had an untidy mop of gingerish hair, and was more wholesome than beautiful to look at, but there was something attractive in her parted lips and very white teeth. Mannering managed to smile, and go on: "May I come down?"

"Who —" the woman began, and her hold tightened on her son, who announced:

"*Man.*"

"Quite a nice man, really," Mannering tried to reassure the woman.

"You — you stay up there until I'm in the house," she ordered. "Benny, come with me." She gave the child no choice but hoisted him up in her arms and first backed, then turned and scurried away.

Mannering waited until she had disappeared before letting his legs dangle over the edge of the flat roof. He saw now that there were such outbuildings attached to all the houses, he was probably sitting over a kitchen or scullery. A rainwater tub stood a few feet along to the left. He edged towards it and lowered himself feet first. His left ankle took the strain without any twinges of pain, his right was slightly painful. But soon he stood upright by the barrel, testing his ankle and deciding that he wasn't really hurt. When he walked towards the gate through which his assailant had passed, he felt quite comfortable.

He looked up and down the alley which had once been

paved with macadam now broken into patches. There were ruts, big holes, some rubble which had been rolled into some of the holes, a dispiriting prospect altogether. He turned left, towards the nearer end, and when he reached the street beyond turned left and left again. Each one was very like Riston Street.

Mannering turned into Riston Street at last.

A crowd of fifty or sixty people had gathered near Number 17. In the middle, it seemed, was a policeman's helmet, and as Mannering appeared at one end a police car appeared at the other. The old man was at the gate. On the other side of the road Doris Paget stood holding her baby, surrounded by neighbours, and Clive Paget was on the fringe of the crowd outside Number 17. As Mannering drew nearer he saw through the bobbing heads that Julie was talking to the policeman.

Mannering's station wagon was close by.

It would be easy to get into this and drive off but that would only postpone the time of questioning. It might worry Julie, too, for she would wonder what had happened to him. And it might also imply that he did not want it to be known that he was involved. So he passed the wagon, as Doris Paget pointed at him, excitedly. Paget was now in the thick of the crowd and as Mannering reached the fringe, the other man called out:

"What's up, Julie? Did Mannering give you trouble?" His voice was loud and blustering. "If he did —"

Julie stated simply: "Someone tried to kill him."

"Kill *Mannering*?"

"Yes. He —"

"Now, miss," interpolated the constable, a youthful-looking man. "I shouldn't talk too much if I were you."

"Did you see who it was?" demanded Paget.

"Now, sir —" began the policeman. Then he saw that his reinforcements had arrived, and he placed a hand on the girl's shoulder. "We'd better get inside, miss." His voice took on a stern note. "Clear a path, please, clear a path."

Men from the car pushed their way through and the

crowd began to make way for Julie and the policeman, but as Julie turned she caught sight of Mannering, spun round and out of the policeman's grasp and ran to Mannering, arms outstretched.

"Oh, you're safe," she cried. "Thank God, you're safe!"

Next moment she was huddled against him, arms bent between them; and she began to cry. Even as he stood with his arms about her, protectively, and with every eye now turned towards him, Mannering was acutely aware that she had turned to him as a girl might turn to her lover.

Not her brother, not her father, not simply a friend; but as if he meant everything in the world to her.

And he could feel her sobbing.

6

Suicide or Not?

AT LEAST A HUNDRED people were gathered about them
on that instant, and except to turn and look at him, none
moved : not even the two policemen from the car. The
grey-haired, bent old man was glaring, Clive Paget looked
astounded, and from the gate of Number 20 came a voice
which Mannering felt sure was Doris Paget's.

"Look ! She *knows* him."

The policeman from whom Julie had broken loose was
frowning, as if anxious to establish his authority but not
sure how to. The scene was set like a tableau for no more
than thirty seconds and perhaps only ten or fifteen; but it
was etched like a chiselled sculpture on the back of
Mannering's mind.

Without a moment's warning he lifted Julie in his arms,
and stepped forward. The crowd parted like the Red Sea,
and closed behind him as he reached the gate. The bent old
man, a liver-spotted hand on the iron bar, pulled it open;
it was still creaking as Mannering swept past; or did the
creaks come from those dry bones? Mannering stepped
into the now familiar passage and up the now familiar
stairs, his shoulder pressed against the wall, Julie's head
resting in the crook of his arm and her hair falling over
the banisters. Her eyes were open and tears were in them.
He carried her past the open bathroom door, and caught
a glimpse of the hanging noose. Then he went into the
front room, and for a moment stood and contemplated the
unconscious man on the bed.

Tom Forrester hadn't stirred; he still lay on his back with his pointed chin, his arched nose, making him look like one of the devil's angels.

Mannering bent down and placed Julie gently on to the bed, then backed away.

H₋ felt a few twinges of pain in his right shoulder and the slightest of pain in his right ankle, but otherwise was little the worse for wear. But he felt very tired. He cleared one of the upright chairs of oddments, a bra and two pairs of panty-hose, a slip and some folded shirts, and sat down as the youthful-looking policeman who was faintly reminiscent of James Stewart and had the same kind of figure, appeared at the doorway. Immediately and earnestly, he asked:

"You *are* Mr. John Mannering, sir, aren't you?"

"Yes," said Mannering.

"Of Quinns?" The young man meant to be in no doubt at all.

"Of Quinns," Mannering confirmed, seeing another policeman turn the head of the stairs and glance to his right — into the bathroom. He stopped on the instant and exclaimed:

"What the —" and then his voice tailed off.

"Do you mind telling me what you're doing here?" the earnest young man asked, with a half-glance at Julie, so still on the bed.

"I came to see Mr. Forrester's paintings," Mannering replied.

"*Jack,*" called the policeman by the bathroom, "*have you seen this?*"

"Mr. Forrester's paintings, sir?"

"Yes. This flat is full of them. I —"

"*Jack,*" called the policeman behind the policeman, "*come and take a look at this.*"

A querulous voice sounded from downstairs: "They're all the same, them hippies. Kill you as lief as look at you, they would."

"Jack —"

The earnest police constable said, on the turn, "You won't go away, sir, will you?" as if Mannering would leave by the window the moment his back was turned. Without waiting for reassurance he joined his colleague in the tiny hall, and looked into the bathroom. Immediately he exclaimed as if what he now saw drove thought of everything else out of his mind.

"Good God!"

"The quicker we tell H.Q. about this affair the better," said the policeman from the car, and he pulled his walkie-talkie radio from his breast pocket. Whatever he said was on a low key, and although Mannering knew he was talking, he had no idea what was being said.

He himself looked long and thoughtfully at Julie, and eventually he asked:

"How are you feeling?"

"Awful," she replied.

"I can believe it. Did you get a good look at the man?"

"I hardly saw him at all, I just knew he was there, trying to —" she broke off, with a shudder. "Are you all right?"

"Yes, thanks."

"Did the man get away?"

"Over the roofs, yes."

"You — you might have broken your neck," Julie said, reproach quite apparent in her voice.

"Or I might have been hanged by it," he retorted.

"Oh, please!" She drew in her breath, hissingly.

"Julie, did you know anyone was up there?"

"Good gracious, no!"

"All right," he said, hoping against hope that that was true. "Now answer this. Why did you and Tom really come to see me? Was it because of the paintings, his art for art's sake —" he could not keep the contempt out of his voice — "or was it because he was in fear of his life, in fear of being murdered? Did he come hoping for help because of that?"

She was looking at him as if horrified, but did not

answer, and Mannering went on in a very harsh but low-pitched voice :

"Did he really try to commit suicide, Julie? Or did someone try to murder him? Did you know his life was in danger. Let's have the whole truth now. What are the pair of you up to?"

And as he put that question, he could picture her in his mind's eye as she flung herself into his arms as into the arms of a lover.

Julie did not answer immediately. Mannering had a feeling that she was taken completely by surprise, and badly shocked. She looked older, but perhaps that was because she was exhausted. Yet did that elfin face have a cunning expression? And was she surprised because he had penetrated a wall of pretence which she and Tom had built? Had they visited him because he was in danger and had he felt this was a coward's way out and been so arrogant and resentful because she had persuaded him against his inclination and his own better judgment?

The policeman finished on his walkie-talkie. The door of this bedroom was open but there was no way of telling what the foot patrol policeman had overheard. The pair of them exchanged glances as the one with the radio moved forward.

"The C.I.D. is on its way, Mr. Mannering."

"That's just as well," Mannering approved.

"What did happen, sir?"

He could demur, saying that there was no point in telling his story twice, but these men would want to make their own reports as zesty as they could. It was always wise to have the goodwill of the men on the local beat, so he said, simply :

"I came to see the paintings, and when I got here, it looked as if Mr. Forrester had tried to hang himself. The young lady had managed to get him down, and save his life. When I went to look round a man in the attic dropped the noose over my head. I managed to slip out

of it, and he ran away over the roofs." Mannering paused,
smiling wryly. "He was younger and sprightlier than I,
and got away."

The men's eyes were generous in obvious admiration.
Mannering sensed their impulse to ask more questions, but
they mastered it. Soon, there were the sounds of a car
outside, doors slammed, a man called out : "Make way,
please make way." Almost at once footsteps sounded on
the porch and in the passage and on the stairs. The two
uniformed men turned to the men from the Criminal
Investigation Department, and this gave Mannering and
the girl a few moments' respite.

"I want the answer, Julie — did you come to me to get
help because Tom was under threat? Or was it really for
help with the pictures? I need to know and the police
may have to, soon."

She eased herself up, leaning on one elbow, and stretched a hand towards him in obvious appeal.

"Please," she breathed. "Don't tell the police."

"Why did you come to me?" insisted Mannering.
"Hurry, or they'll have to know."

"For both reasons," she burst out, her strength of feeling
making it difficult to keep her voice low. "I'll tell you
everything when we have the chance, but please don't
tell the police." Now she got to her knees and stretched
out both arms, again as to a lover. And she repeated,
pleadingly : "*Please* don't tell the police."

Her voice faded away as two men in plain clothes
moved across the tiny, crowded landing and into this
room. Both were in their early thirties, Mannering judged.
One was tall and fair-haired and fresh complexioned,
with the look of a man from the countryside; the other
was leaner and severe-looking, dark-haired, thin-faced
and sharp featured but not at all like Tom Forrester
despite the colouring and the aquiline nose and chin.

He came into the room first.

"I am Detective Sergeant Joslin, sir, of the Criminal
Investigation Department, from the Hammersmith

Divisional Headquarters." He glanced at Julie, and then more protractedly at Forrester. "Is anyone here in need of medical attention?"

"I don't think so," Mannering answered.

"In that case, I would like to ask some questions. First, your name and address, please."

Mannering gave it, solemnly, before telling the story of what had happened, even including the visit to Quinns and so his reason for coming to Fulham. The only point he did not raise was the doubt about Forrester's suicide bid; they would soon begin to suspect that it might have been attempted murder. Even as he talked and the rustic-looking officer took copious notes in shorthand, Mannering wondered more and more why Julie should be so anxious not to tell the police that she — and presumably her Tom — had been frightened lest Tom might be murderously attacked.

At last, he finished.

Almost without a pause, the dark-haired policeman turned to Julie, and asked without a change of tone: "Now may I have your name, please?"

She hesitated. She coloured. She sat up on the bed next to Tom, and answered quietly but without hesitation and without a quiver in her voice:

"My name is Julie Clarendon, and this is my address."

Tom Forrester lay so still, not watching, not hearing; and both of the detectives as well as the uniformed policeman, looked beyond Julie to the man. As policemen they had no moral duties, had simply to take down what facts they knew, and to find out all that were relevant. But as men —

Mannering had the impression that they were all sorry for the girl but had no time at all for Forrester.

Julie told her story, which coincided so accurately with Mannering's that it was almost a carbon copy. Why the police had allowed her to listen to his statement there was no way of telling, but it eased the situation, and when she had finished she looked much less tense and worried. The detective sergeant relaxed, smiled, and remarked:

"Do you feel nervous, Miss Clarendon?"

"Yes," she answered.

"We'll have men on duty for the rest of the night," Joslin said. "And when Mr. Forrester comes round we can find out from him what really happened. You'll be in London, won't you, Mr. Mannering?"

"Yes," Mannering answered. "And I'd better be going." He turned to Julie and promised again: "If I can help Tom I will. And just in case you need my home address —" he took a card from his inside breast pocket and handed it to her. "If I'm not in, my wife will almost certainly be. Good night, Julie."

"Good night," she echoed.

And she put her face up, to be kissed.

Mannering was smiling crookedly when he went down the stairs, but was brought sharply back to consider the more public aspect of the situation. Thirty or more people were still hanging about, half of them in their early teens. Paget had gone but his wife, no longer carrying the baby, was among the crowd. A policeman stood in the doorway, and wished Mannering good night as Mannering went towards his car. Immediately, camera lights flashed and two other men levelled cameras, while a man with a nearly bald head moved from the side of the station wagon.

"Good evening, Mr. Mannering. Had some excitements, I'm told."

"Great excitements," Mannering agreed, for it would be ill-advised to make the Press hostile. "I came to see Tom Forrester's paintings and someone tried to choke the life out of me with a noose at the end of a rope . . . Yes, of course you can quote me . . . No, I hadn't seen either of them — Julie or Tom Forrester . . . until they came to Quinns today . . . They wanted me to sponsor Forrester, whom they both hope is a genius . . . I don't even begin to know whether he is or not . . . I didn't have much time to look but some of the paintings are interesting . . . I've no idea at all why I was attacked and can't dream one up . . . . Was I hurt? A scratch or two, that's all, the most painful one was a splinter in a finger." He held his hand up and extended the finger as far as he could. "Anyone like a photograph?" There was a general chuckle and one camera-light flashed. Mannering joined in the laughter, and went on : "Now I'd like to go and have my dinner, if you don't mind. Good night."

He climbed into the car and drove off, suddenly aware that it was nearly half-past eight, and Lorna would have been expecting him for an hour at least. He should have telephoned to tell her he was late. He paused impatiently at the corner of this street and Wandsworth Bridge Road, then swung left. He lived less than ten minutes drive away, in Chelsea not far from the Embankment and not far from King's Road. So there was no point in stopping to tele- phone.

As he turned, he saw Clive Paget approaching in his bright green M.G. on the near side of the road.

Lorna Mannering thought, he can't be much longer, surely.

She was in the kitchen of the Mannering's apartment at the top of an old Georgian house in Green Street, Chelsea, one of two standing after a night of bombing during the war. Now there were new houses to the right of them and small blocks of flats which looked like bee- hives to the back, and buildings of all kinds surrounding them, but none too close. Since some old buildings had been demolished for a new housing project, there was a distant view of trees, spreading their bright foliage wide, and even on the far side of the river.

She wore a bottle green housecoat which fell almost to her ankles, and was slim-waisted with more than a touch of elegance. Her dark hair, with a few streaks of grey, was drawn back in wings from her forehead. She was a strikingly handsome woman, and the years touched her

with dignity. Her grey eyes were very clear, her complexion very good indeed.

She had water boiling for spring greens and new
potatoes, and a small joint of stuffed veal in the oven,
sizzling very slightly. She normally put the vegetables on
when John came in, for they would cook while he had
a wash or a shower and a drink. The veal would taste
none the worse for being overdone, and her only concern
was for John. It was rare for him to be in later than
half-past six unless he telephoned beforehand. Now, it
was nearly half-past eight. If she didn't hear very soon
she would put in a call to Bristow.

She went into the small study, where they usually had
a pre-dinner drink, and coffee and brandy afterwards. It
was a panelled room with dark oak furniture, mostly
Jacobean, each piece a gem. Two Dutch panels, one by
Vermeer, were over a fireplace so intricately carved that
it seemed more Italian than English, although the carving
had been done by monks of an Abbey long since fallen
into decay.

For years past they had managed, happily, without a
living-in maid. They had a good daily who would come
soon after Lorna had prepared breakfast, so that Lorna
could go up to the attic studio which was six times as
large as the one in Riston Street — the one Lorna did
not know. She enjoyed cooking dinner, enjoyed the quiet
evenings which usually followed; theirs had become a very
happy life although for a brief and alarming spell a few
years ago grave emotional dangers had threatened.

That kind of danger was unthought-of, now.

So, she consoled herself, were most others. While months
would pass without threat of violence, without circumstances goading John into action which might mean
conflict with the police, or else lead to the physical danger
which John scoffed at but she took very seriously indeed.

Nothing could have happened out of the blue, could it?
she worried herself. A small porcelain French clock surrounded by angels in the study chimed, and she watched it

as she moved towards the telephone. I'll call Bill right away, she thought, and on that instant, the front door bell rang, and she changed her direction and her pace and went at once to answer it. Until then she had been aware of danger, but the everyday commonplace of the door-bell ringing drove thought of it out of her mind. She even thought, with a glow of relief, that John might have forgotten his keys; it wouldn't be the first time he had left them at Quinns.

She opened the door.

A man stood there with a stocking drawn over his head and face, and with a gun in his hand. As she tried to slam the door on him, he stuck his foot out so that it swung back on her. Then he pushed her roughly aside, stepped in and closed the door.

"You've got the Fiora jewels here," he stated in a hoarse voice from behind the grotesque mask. "I want them. And I'll get them or I'll kill you. Don't make any mistake about that."

7

Thief

LORNA BACKED INTO THE hall, and the man followed, the gun only a few inches away from her. She could not see his features because they were so squashed by the stocking but she could sense his menace and felt that he wasn't lying; if he didn't get what he wanted he would kill her.

He kicked the door to with his heel.

"Come on," he said. "Give."

She knew, with an awful sense of hopelessness, that the Fiora jewels were not here.

The police knew they were back in London and were on the 'market', but John had not bought them and they were not at the flat.

But would the man believe her?

Heart thumping, breath coming in shallow gasps, she watched him. Suddenly he raised his free hand and slapped her across the face. The blow stung. She staggered to one side and put out a hand to support herself against the wall, as he caught her other hand and twisted the wrist painfully.

"Come on," he repeated. "Where are they?"

What could she say even to gain time? *And what could she do even if she gained it?* She searched desperately for some kind of answer, and suddenly one came; one which he might conceivably believe.

"I only know where they might be," she said, and her tongue clove to the roof of her mouth, the words merging with one another.

"Don't mumble!" he rasped. "What did you say?"

She felt so utterly alone, and so afraid. There was no hope of help. nothing could be done unless she did it herself, and she did not know what she could possibly do. She repeated what she had said very slowly and deliberately, although she had never known her tongue or her lips more dry.

"I only know where they might be."

"What the hell do you mean by that?" He twisted her wrist again, and the pain made her gasp. "Play it straight or you'll be sorry."

The mask pressed tight against his mouth and nose, squashing them. It squeezed his hair and his eyebrows, his cheeks and his chin. It was as if she were looking at a half-formed creature who would never become old. But the fine nylon did not press against his eyelashes or his eyes. The lashes were short, black, stubby, and his eyes might be any colour with the pale stocking superimposed but there was a scar on the pupil of one of them; on the pupil itself. She would never fail to recognise it, a tiny little white dot about the size of a pin-head.

If she lived

"My — my husband didn't tell me he had the Fiora jewels here," she said.

"That's a bloody lie!"

"If you won't believe what I tell you, what is the use of my saying anything?" she demanded.

She thought he was going to strike her again. His jerky manner and gasped sentences made it seem as if he were so much on edge that he could hardly control himself. The grip on her arm tightened, but he actually backed a pace.

"You know where he would put them, don't you?"

"I only know of one hiding place here," she said.

He let her go but gave her a little shove and ordered: "Show me!"

Very slowly, she turned round. There *was* only one place where John would conceal valuables, unless he were deliberately hiding them from her; that was in the settle in his study. As this realisation came she began to recover from the shock, and her mind began to work more freely. Several things became certain.

John had not brought the Fiora jewels here, or he would have told her.

There were other jewels, some being held for customers at Quinns as well as her own jewellery, in the settle, which was a carefully disguised safe and had to be opened with a key. She had a key, but this man didn't know that she had, and it would hardly be surprising if Mannering kept it with him.

As these thoughts ran through her mind, the man was breathing very hard. He had hurried to get here, and in his way was as nervous as she. If she were careful, *very* careful, she could outwit him. But if she failed then she had little doubt that he would kill her.

All of these things passed through her mind as she moved towards the study. There, the soft lights from wall fittings glowed on the dark panels, on the furniture, on the decanters and the glasses standing by John's chair; on the leather pouffe she liked to sit on.

"Where?" hissed the man behind her.

She pointed to the settle : "In there. He —"

"Get the other end of it," he ordered. "Where I can keep my eye on you." He motioned to her with the gun. *"Go on!"*

She did exactly what he told her, and keeping the gun covering her, he crouched down to get at the settle.

"How does it open?"

"The seat's open now," she told him.

"Don't talk to me about an unlocked safe !"

"The safe is built into the bottom," she told him, which was the simple truth.

Very slowly, still gasping for breath, still covering her, he went down on one knee and put the fingers of his free hand on the over-lapping ledge of the settle. He tried the seat, and it moved, and she sensed new tension grow in him. He raised the seat up slowly, and let it rest against the back of the settle.

"Don't you move!" He thrust the gun closer her, then looked into the settle. All he could see were big books, bound in calf. They were press-cuttings books containing cuttings spread over twenty or more years : cuttings about the John who had been, so long ago, and later, cuttings about Quinns. Recently, two more had been added : press notices about her, Lorna's, early paintings.

In all there were nine books, and before anyone could get at the fitted safe, each book had to be taken out.

"What the hell's this?" the man cried, swivelling round and thrusting the gun forward.

And as she had expected, he kept his free hand on the edge of the seat.

Here was her chance! Her heart thumped in dread lest she should fail, but the moment was here and she dare not let it pass. He was glaring up into her face, and all she had to do was move her left hand a few inches and tip the hinged seat forward on to his fingers.

"Wha — what do you mean?" she managed to say.

"These are old books! This isn't a safe!"

"The books are on top of the safe," she said with difficulty, and moved her hand as if to show what she meant; she was only an inch from the seat, and his hand still rested on the edge. "Look, the safe's at the bottom."

He stared at her in a kind of hatred, then glanced into the settle. As he did so, she tipped the seat forward with her fingers. It made no sound as it fell but it seemed an age before it toppled. Even if he snatched his hand away he would be off balance if not hurt and she would still have a chance.

The seat fell, missing his forehead by inches. But for the stocking mask he might have seen the shadow. He simply peered into the settle and the seat struck his fingers with crushing force. There was a split-second of silence, before the pain spread through his hand and arm and body.

He screamed.

And he pulled the trigger, as Lorna darted to one side.

The gun flashed and barked, the bullet hit one of the panels with a cracking, splintering sound. Then the man pulled his hand away and reeled about the room, still holding the gun but having no control of it. She could try to snatch it from him; instead, she ran to the door and into the hall, slammed the door and turned the key in the lock. She could hear her prisoner gasping, swearing, screeching, roaring. She leaned against the door, knowing that she was safe, and suddenly she began to shiver from head to foot.

She did not hear the front door open or see Mannering stride in.

As the small lift stopped at the top floor, Mannering felt quite relaxed and content. He had made the journey in less than ten minutes, and in a few seconds he would see Lorna and there would be the deep pleasure of that as well as the relief of knowing that she had no cause for anxiety. Before long he would be in a warm bath, he needed that to ease the aches and bruises; then he would relax with a whisky-and-soda, with Lorna sitting on the pouffe while he related those events of the day he thought it wise for her to hear.

The lift door slid open, with hardly a sound.

He heard the crack of a shot.

It came as he was poised to go forward. It stopped him in his tracks, sending alarm screaming through him, but that was only a momentary pause before he plunged forward, caught his foot as the door began to close, digging into his pocket as he staggered forward, taking out his keys.

He thought : Oh, dear God !

He heard no footsteps, which would surely have sounded had a man rushed towards the door.

He selected the right Yale key with great care, thrust it into the key hole, then flung the door back and strode inside.

The first sight gave a moment of relief, followed by swift, searing fear. Lorna was leaning against the study door, head drooping, body shivering; and he thought she must be hurt. Shot? He moved swiftly towards her, then heard the man beyond the door, swearing and groaning. He reached Lorna and put his arms round her, and at once she raised her head; at least there was no outward sign of injury. Her teeth were chattering and her body still shaking, but her eyes were open wide, almost staring.

"He — he's got a gun," she muttered.

"Are you hurt?" Mannering made himself say.

"No. Just — just scared. *He's got a gun.*"

"Yes, I heard," Mannering said. "He sounds —" he broke off, put his arms more closely about her waist and shoulders and led her away from the door. "Wait in the kitchen."

"John, be careful! He's armed!"

"I'll be careful," Mannering promised.

Above the sounds of the man's swearing and moaning there came the roar of a shot, and the study door quivered as a bullet burst through it just above the lock. A second earlier and it would have struck Lorna at waist height. Mannering half-pushed, half-carried her to the kitchen and spun round as another shot roared. This time the door sagged, the ancient lock shattered by the two bullets. Mannering flattened himself against the wall as the man inside kicked the door open. He still held the gun. He still had the stocking over his head. He was glaring and staring, as he said :

"Where are you, you bitch?"

He saw the kitchen door wide open and Lorna's shadow there. Quite unaware of Mannering he moved towards the kitchen, his gun outstretched. Mannering simply put his hand forward, clutched and twisted the wrist, and made the gun fall. The intruder swivelled round in alarm and Mannering, filled with cold anger, struck him first with his right fist and then with his left, one blow on and one beneath the jaw. The man staggered back several paces, and then fell like a felled tree.

He did not stir.

Mannering turned, to see Lorna in the kitchen doorway. She was standing upright and the shivering fit had passed. Mannering went to her, held her shoulders, scanned her face which was now very pale, and leaned forward and kissed her on the forehead. Gently he led her back to the kitchen which was white and primrose yellow, with a glossy black rocking-chair. He pulled this forward and steadied her as she sat down, said "Don't move, darling," then opened a dresser drawer and took out a ball of picture cord, white flecked with red. He cut off a length with a carving knife, then went out to the intruder, who lay flat on his back. Mannering hoisted him up, dragged him to an upright chair near the door, dumped him in and tied him to it, with cord round his waist. Then he tied his wrists together, behind his back, and did a reef knot.

The man would not come round for five minutes or more, and even when fully conscious wouldn't have a chance to free himself.

Mannering stood looking down, actually moved his hand forward to take off the stocking, decided that Lorna needed attention first and crossed quickly to the kitchen.

"Brandy?" he asked.

"John, I'd love a cup of coffee," she said, huskily.

"Instantly done," Mannering assured her, and plugged in an electric kettle. "I could do with a whisky-and-soda!" He went out, brought back both decanters then poured out his drink, made instant coffee, and laced it with brandy. Lorna, her colour returning, sipped it slowly and with obvious pleasure. For the first time Mannering sat down and watched her as he drank. She had always been beautiful, with her slightly arched black eyebrows, her high forehead, her full lips; and she seemed to grow more beautiful with the years.

"How long had he been here?" he asked at last.

"About ten minutes, I suppose."

"How did you manage to lock him in?"

She told him enough for him to be able to fill in the gaps : of her fear and her courage and her desperation, as well as her quick-thinking and her ingenuity. And she told him that the man had thought that he had the Fiora jewels and had brought them here.

"They are not," Mannering said quite definitely. "I know they're on the market, but that's all. And this joker came right out of the blue, you say."

"Yes," Lorna answered. "He gave me no warning at all. I was just about to ring Bristow because you were so late. John, wha — *John*! You've got a bruise on your forehead, and your cheek's scratched!"

She broke off, with belated alarm for him, while an aircraft roared, very low, one of the few nuisance noises common in this flat. She pushed the rocking-chair back and bent over Mannering, looking for more evidence of injury, and he began to tease and laugh at her, a measure of his great relief.

In the midst of this, and without any warning, there was a click of sound outside; the closing of the front door.

"He's got away!" cried Mannering, and sprang to his feet and rushed to the hall, with Lorna just behind him.

But the man was still sitting where Mannering had left him; head drooping, chin on chest, body slumped forward, legs stretched out. Behind him the door was firmly closed, while a sound of the closing of the lift doors came clearly through the quiet.

8

Knife Wound

MANNERING REACHED THE HALL door, placed his fingers on
the handle, and then drew back. He couldn't reach the
bottom floor before the man in the lift, so there was no
sense at all in following whoever had been there but every
reason for seeing what he looked like. So he spun round,
and Lorna backed away. "Camera," he breathed and ran
into the big drawing room which was on the right of the
front door and had windows overlooking the street. The
room was in Regency style, which Lorna loved, and it
was Lorna's décor, the curtains on brass rails drawn well
back from the windows.

He reached one window, threw it up, and peered out.

Several people were in the street, two cars were moving
towards each other, a traffic warden, off duty, was getting
out of a red Morris 1100. No one appeared to look up.
Lorna was suddenly by his side, a small Leica in her hand,
and she turned the lenses and then gave it to him.

"It's on the right focus," she said.

He leaned further out, poising the camera on the pavement just below the window. For a few moments he feared
that the man — if it had been a man — might have left
the building already, but no — there he was.

He looked young, and he had long hair and wore jeans.

He stepped briskly towards King's Road, his back to
Mannering, who focused the camera just ahead of the
youth and pressed the catch as the other came into sight.

Then suddenly the man turned and looked round and upwards. For a moment his head and face appeared in the camera sight, and Mannering snapped again.

"With luck I've got a good one," he said thankfully.

The youth saw him, too, swung round and began to hurry, then broke into a run as if he couldn't control his fear of being followed. He ran round the corner without another glance, as Lorna leaned out, shoulder to shoulder with Mannering.

"I wonder what *he* wanted," she said.

"The Fioras, probably," Mannering said, drawing back from the window. "I wish —" he broke off, and for a moment was very still, so still and obviously alarmed that Lorna turned to look over her shoulder as if she feared someone else was there.

Only the sitting prisoner was in sight, and he hadn't moved.

Mannering said, quite clearly : "Fool. Oh, what a fool." He put a hand on Lorna's arm, and went on : "I mean, I am." He took half a dozen long strides towards the man, and very cautiously tipped his head up by placing a finger beneath his chin.

The eyes were partly open; the mouth was slack.

Mannering felt for his pulse, as he had for Tom Forrester's not so very long ago, and found it utterly still. There was no sign of breathing, either. He looked slowly over the top of the prisoner's head and saw the dark stain on the pale, washed-out blue of the shirt. It was beneath the left shoulder, crimson, and spreading. He drew back and turned to Lorna, took her hand, and said :

"Now we have no choice at all. We must send for the police."

"So he — is dead?" She was not greatly surprised.

"Yes," Mannering said. "Now it's a clear case of murder, whereas until now it was only murder attempted." H went back to the kitchen and finished the whisky-and-soda looked out of the back window, and went on : "I could d with an hour's rest, but we can hardly sit here and eat with the body out there."

Lorna eyed him levelly: "What you really mean is that you need time to think."

"You're right in one," Mannering admitted, but at once stretched out for the telephone, which stood on a ledge near the big refrigerator. "But I can't have it!" He dialled Bristow's number, in Putney, but there was no answer, so he began to dial Westminster 1212, the New Yard number, and had to wait only for a moment. When the operator at Scotland Yard answered, he asked mechanically: "Is Superintendent Bristow there?" and then snapped his fingers in vexation and went on before the operator spoke again: "I mean, whoever has taken Mr. Bristow's place."

"I can give you *Information*," the woman said.

"Yes," said Mannering. "That's the best thing." It was nearly thirty years since he had first known Bristow as his contact at Scotland Yard; habit died slowly. Lorna was placing cup and saucer and glass to go into the dishwasher, behaving quite normally although probably not yet out of shock of the break-in, of the danger, and now this sudden death.

"Information," a man said.

"This is John Mannering," Mannering began.

"Good evening, Mr. Mannering." The voice was familiar but Mannering couldn't place the man. "You had some bother at Fulham tonight, I gather." There was a hint of laughter in the other's tone.

"And now there's more trouble at Chelsea," Mannering told him.

"Not serious, I hope."

"Just a little case of murder," announced Mannering evenly.

"*Is* it, sir! Then I'll get a car over at once — are you at Green Street?"

"Yes."

"I'll send a car over at once, and also inform Chief Inspector Willison, who is in charge of the incident at

Fulham. You'll stay there until our men arrive, sir, won't you?"

"Nothing would move me," Mannering assured him. "May I know your name?"

"Chief Inspector Fell, sir," the other replied, and immediately brought a picture of a youthful, sandy-haired man with lively eyes, who had once been at one of the divisional headquarters in the south-west of London.

"Oh, I remember. So you're now in charge of *Information*."

"By nights, sir. Yes."

"Nice to have a friend at court," responded Mannering, and rang off.

Lorna had been busy most of the time behind him. As he turned she was cutting through some appetising-looking beef sandwiches, and put them on plates on a tray — twice as many for him as for her. Next she opened the refrigerator door and took out a can of beer and put it on the shiny kitchen table.

"It won't help if you're famished," she remarked.

"No. What were we going to have?"

"Roast veal," she replied.

"Roast veal," Mannering repeated, and looked bleakly at the door and the hall beyond. "Cold tomorrow." He moved his chair so that he could look out of the window, into the blue sky with a few fleecy clouds as well as two vapour trails which made a long-tailed cross which furred out slowly and gradually merged into the colour of the sky. "Lorna, my love, we aren't going to be able to talk much for a while. You know what it's like when the police take-over. Did the man go into the bedroom or in here?"

"No."

"Then we may be able to stay from under their feet," Mannering said. "Darling —"

There was a ring at the front door bell, and he put a half-eaten sandwich on a plate and slid off his stool.

"They've been quick," he said, and went to open the front door.

But it wasn't the police : it was Bill Bristow.

"John," said Bristow, "one of the senior officers at Fulham called and told me what was going on, and that Willison is in charge of the investigation and is treating it as attempted murder." So far Mannering was between him and the dead man, and he hadn't seen the body. "So I thought I should fill you in about Willison as soon as I could."

"A *very* good idea," Mannering approved, gratefully.

"I thought you'd think so. Willison is probably the best man at the Yard on art thefts. He has a far better technical knowledge than most about painters and periods and schools of art. But otherwise he is a cold fish. He won't be either friendly or hostile where you are concerned but will keep you guessing, and most of the time you'll guess that he can't wait to clap the darbies on you."

Lorna said in vexation : "That's *just* the man we need now."

Bristow looked at her over Mannering's shoulder.

"Hallo Lorna. I —" then broke off, obviously astounded as he glimpsed the man in the chair.

"Bill," Mannering urged, "get out while you can. I may need some help but if you're here when the Yard chaps come, you probably won't be able to get away. I'm anxious to find out all I can about the couple at Fulham, especially if there's any known motive for an attempt on Forrester's life." He spoke with a tone of urgency and stretched out his hand to open the door. "Oh — and about the Fioras," he added.

Bristow asked sharply : "Why the Fioras?"

"This man thought I had them here," explained Mannering and opened the door.

"The Yard has two or three pieces from the collection," Bristow said, "and the present theory is that they've been held for years by a private collector who was interested only in possessing them; and have recently been stolen from him. No one knows names or anything else. You could call it an intelligent guess."

That was all Mannering needed to know for the time being.

The landing was empty and a lighted Number 5 above the lift door showed that the car was still at this floor. Bristow pressed the button and stepped inside as the door opened. As it closed on him, he looked very worried, obviously wishing that he had time to hear more, probably wishing he could be present when the police arrived.

He vanished from sight.

"John," Lorna said, in a helpless voice. "What *has* been going on? What's all this about Fulham?"

Briskly, Mannering answered: "A frustrated artist, a patient mistress, a bathroom and an attic full of some saucy and some erotic pictures, an attempt to kill him or an attempt at suicide. A man had a crack at me, too, and I chased him over the roof. This might be the man," he added, and bent down to examine the dead man's shoes and jeans.

There were scratches at the toes, brick dust, two jagged and freshly made tears on the knees. The man's roughened hands were badly grazed and some of his fingernails recently broken and torn; Mannering had little doubt that this was the man he had chased over the roof. The fingers of the left hand were heavily bruised and the skin was split across the knuckles: this was where the seat of the settle had crashed down on him.

"Is he your man?" Lorna asked.

"I don't think there's much doubt."

"John —"

"Darling?"

"What is the connection between this artist and the Fiora jewels?"

"That's a *very* important question," Mannering replied.

"You mean, you don't know?" Lorna asked.

It was not only a question: it was an accusation, or at least a clearly expressed suspicion: that in spite of what he had said to her, and in spite of what he had said to Bristow, he might know more than he had admitted about the famous Fioras. He could not blame her. He had been involved so often in cases which had started innocently enough but become dangerous and violent. And she was well aware that sometimes when danger threatened, he tried to keep it from her.

If she had these doubts, the police might have them, too; that was probably why Bristow had hurried round : to try to find out when they were face to face how far Mannering was already committed. He, Mannering, could tell Bristow what to do, but he couldn't tell Lorna.

He smiled at her.

"No, sweetheart," he said. "I don't know anything about the Fioras except that some have appeared on the market, and someone seems to think I have the rest. I do not. I don't know anything about the artist and his sweetie, except that he paints, she supports him because she believes he is a genius. If he lied to me about his reason for coming to see me, he might also have deceived her."

"Why should he have lied to you?" she demanded.

"He might conceivably have wanted to involve me in the rest of the Fioras," Mannering said. "If he did, events defeated him."

He gave this time to sink in, his hazel-brown eyes very clear and teasing and at the same time reassuring. And as she scanned his face as if to reassure herself that he was telling the simple truth, the lift sounded at the landing, and a moment later the front door bell rang. As it echoed, he slid his arms round her, drew her very close, and kissed her full on the lips. Then without a word, he let her go and turned to the front door.

This time, it was Chief Inspector Willison.

Willison was tall and fair, rather Scandinavian to look at, with pale blue eyes and thin lashes; not an albino but much nearer to one than most fair people. His features had a raw look, as if the wind and the sun had burned them and they had never quite healed. He had full, well-shaped lips, but they had a natural twist which made it seem as if he were sneering; or at least, sceptical and derisive. He wore a dark blue suit of conventional cut which threw his blondness into sharp relief, broad shoulders and a rangy figure; and he moved very easily, almost with a cat-like motion. All the time he listened his expression seemed to shower cold particles of doubt on Mannering's story.

He was briskly efficient.

An ambulance arrived; a police surgeon came, soon followed by a murder squad including photographers and fingerprint men. Black marks were made on the floor about the chair, more were made in the study, and fingerprint powder was spread liberally. Willison himself took a quick look into all of the rooms, told his team what to do in the most precise terms, and then left them to get on with the job. He conveyed an impression of ruthless efficiency; also, of ruthlessness.

With him, like a shadow, was a detective sergeant with a shock of black hair and a big bald spot on top; a scientist of a man who had a notebook and pencil and made his notes with casual ease.

"So the man threatened to kill you, Mrs Mannering. Just where were you standing? I see ... And he thought Mr. Mannering had the Fiora Collection ... did you, Mr. Mannering? ... I am very glad to hear it, for we have reason to believe some or all of the collection is on the market again —the unlawful market ... Did the deceased say why he had concluded that your husband had the collection? ... No. You say he, the intruder, appeared to be very nervous ... And you knocked him out, Mr. Mannering. How many blows did you strike? ... I see ... And you left him here before calling the police? ... While calling the police and relaxing, I see. There are perhaps better times to relax than when you have a violent intruder in your flat ... Particularly as the second man broke in and — as we now know — stabbed the first ... Do you know how he broke in? ... He probably picked the lock, I see, and the night

time precautions of chain and bolts weren't in position . . .
I see. You did say you thought he was the man who had
attempted to kill both you and Mr. Forrester in Riston
Street, Fulham, didn't you? . . . So he was an attempted
murder suspect . . . How often have you been to Riston
Street, Mr. Mannering? . . . Your first visit? Really? Then
if you haven't been to visit the young woman Clarendon,
Julie Clarendon, at her home where have you seen her? . . .
You haven't seen her before today? . . . Come, Mr. Mannering, you really cannot expect me to pretend to believe
that even if your wife *is* present."

9

The Icy Inspector

THE LAST WORDS ECHOED in Mannering's mind, as they must in Lorna's. He had no doubt that they were intended to disturb her at least as much as they were to disturb him. From the moment Willison had come he had been coldly aggressive, and his flow of questions and comments, virtually a cross-examination, had been making Mannering not only angry but very wary. Both Lorna and he needed rest. She had suffered a shock which would have lain many women prostrate, and Willison knew this as well as the fact that Mannering had been working at extreme pressure and tension during the past few hours.

Undoubtedly, Willison was pressing them because he knew they were on the point of exhaustion. As certainly, he held some sharp suspicions in reserve and was far from certain that he was being told all the truth. His icy cold manner had a knife-like edge. So had the expression in his eyes as he looked at Mannering without allowing his gaze to flicker towards Lorna. Something in his expression seemed to say : "Ah, I've got you," as he waited for Mannering to reply.

Slowly, very slowly, Mannering smiled : a broad, apparently good-natured smile, which certainly concealed any sign of perturbation.

"You're quite wrong," he stated. "I do expect you to believe me. I expect any man, policeman or not, experienced or not, to assume that I am telling the truth unless he has a very good reason not to believe me." He paused, his smile broadening at the policeman's obvious surprise, and went on : "Have you any reason to believe that I am lying, Chief Inspector?"

Willison tried to recover his ascendancy.

"I am a police officer, and I —"

Mannering's voice sharpened.

"Have you any reason to believe I am lying?"

"I have some reason to doubt whether you have yet told me all you know."

"Inspector!" Mannering's voice became loud and penetrating. All the men in the other rooms stopped and turned their heads. "You are arrogant and offensive, and I want either a sound reason for your assumption that I am lying about Julie Clarendon or an immediate apology."

Willison was suddenly a man at bay.

One of the Fingerprint men coughed; someone else dropped a piece of equipment, which clattered very loudly. The silence seemed to drag on interminably, until Willison drew a deep breath and said with great precision :

"I am sorry, Mr. Mannering. I took too much for granted."

Mannering's voice at once became pleasant and normal. "Let's forget it, shall we?" He moved to Lorna and took her arm. "Unless you've any more questions for my wife, I think she should have something to eat and go to bed." He glanced at Lorna. "You must be tired out."

"I could drop," she admitted.

Willison did not respond immediately. Either he was simmering with resentment about the forced apology or there was something else on his mind. In the room which was being searched movement began again, the tension and the watching was over. Willison moistened his lips, then said with an obvious effort :

"Would it be possible for you and Mrs. Mannering to stay with friends for the night?" His gaze didn't falter but his mouth was set in a manner which reminded Mannering of his earlier aggressiveness, although he was no longer so forceful.

What was in his mind?

"Is that really necessary?" Lorna asked, in a vexatious tone; undoubtedly she had been looking forward to her own bed, to absolute relaxation, and she saw the hope of that vanishing.

"It's not vital and I can't force you to go," Willison said, "but I do advise it. We shall be in and out all night. There will be a lot of noise going on, the telephone will keep ringing. You would be much more comfortable with friends."

He was actually going a pale pink.

Why? Mannering asked himself insistently. What was really in his mind? There was some truth in what he said, but before too long the work should be finished. There was only the study and the front door to examine; Good Lord, it shouldn't take more than a couple of hours. What did Willison really want? He had made his apology, whatever else about the man he wasn't stubborn to a point of adamancy; nor was he too stiff with pride. Yet he was pushing this to a point of another conflict.

A thought flashed into Mannering's mind, and he thought he saw the reason : Willison wanted to search this flat thoroughly : he really believed the Fiora Collection was here! It was on the tip of Mannering's tongue to say this, but he checked the impulse. Other thoughts flashed now, his own manner and his mood changed. He turned to Lorna and said easily :

"I think the Inspector's right, darling, and it will be hours before we can settle down here. We'll go along to the Club, that's handiest now that they allow wives in! I'll telephone them while you change."

"But dinner —" Lorna began.

"The veal is overcooked already," Mannering said, and for a moment was very close to her and his expression stopped the protest on her lips.

"I really am sorry, Mrs. Mannering," Willison said.

"We can hardly blame you for doing your job," Mannering said easily. Willison looked relieved if puzzled, and watched them as Mannering led Lorna to the bedroom, closed the door on her and then crossed to the telephone in the study. "All right for me to use this?" he asked, seeing it already daubed with grey powder for fingerprinting.

"Yes," answered Willison, and turned away.

"Don't go," Mannering checked him. "Have a look at that settle, will you, it's really the safe. The books above are full of press cuttings." He dialled as he spoke and almost immediately a woman answered. "John Mannering," Mannering said. "I wonder if you can find a room for me and my wife tonight, we've been driven out of our home!" He smiled broadly at Willison, who hadn't yet moved towards the settle. "You can — splendid! What time does the restaurant close? . . . Then we should just about make it. Thank you." He replaced the receiver and went to the settle, talking briskly all the time, behaving as if he were on top of the world. So far, the settle hadn't been touched but a man was prising at something in a panel. "Bullet there?" he asked, and then lifted the lid of the settle with one finger. "I mustn't smear the other chap's dabs, must I? Lorna literally took her life in her hands when she made this fall on to his fingers." He stood back, and his tone changed and his expression became bleak and hard. "This man tried to kill her. The man who killed him probably came from the same gang. I won't rest until he's caught and the mystery's solved. I hope you understand that."

Willison said in a grating voice: "Nor will I. But —"

"These press cuttings books are very heavy," Mannering remarked, bending down and lifting one. "Will you —"

"Can I help, sir?" asked the man who was prising the bullet out.

"You keep on with what you're doing," Willison ordered, and bent down for another book. Soon all nine were piled on a small gate-leg table which glowed from years of polishing. Mannering straightened the pile, and then explained:

"The safe's built into the false bottom, and the bottom can't be moved — unless you know the trick — while the seat is up." He lowered the seat and then pressed at some of the carving on the back; there was a slight crack of sound.

He raised the seat again, and when they looked down part of the inside had moved, revealing the lock of a modern safe. "I had that lock specially made, but the secret panel came with the monks who made the settle three hundred years ago," he went on, taking his keys from his pocket. He selected one and turned it in the lock; it moved a brass plate aside so that another, smaller, keyhole showed; he used a second key on this and then pulled at the handle which was set in the top of the safe. "*Open sesame*," he said lightly, and had to pull hard. "I've had a million pounds worth of jewels here several times," Mannering said. "Now it contains only my wife's personal jewellery, some documents and, as you see, my will."

He stood back.

Willison looked into the settle at a dozen small cases, all of black or red leather. The Fioras would have taken up every inch of the safe and much more besides. Mannering leaned forward again and took out two of the cases. "I may as well check that they're all here," he said musingly, and, opening them, handed both to Willison and then took out the others. An emerald necklace; emerald ear-rings, rubies in lovely settings were here, none of them wildly extravagant. "Thanks," he said, as he put them back. "If our dead friend was looking for Fioras he would have been very disappointed with these, wouldn't he?"

And he looked straight into Willison's eyes.

"No doubt he would," Willison agreed. "Is that the only safe here?"

"Yes," Mannering answered, standing back again. "Now it's all yours to examine. At one time I kept a lot of jewels here and not at the shop, but now I use the strong room there and seldom bring anything home." Again his tone and his expression changed, and he said grimly : "It is too dangerous for my wife."

"I quite understand," Willison said. "One thing, Mr. Mannering."

"Yes?"

"Where will you be tonight?"

"The Eighteenth Century Club in Eton Square."

"Thank you." Now Willison braced himself, and Mannering knew that a question of much greater importance was coming; and Willison seemed to have some difficulty in bringing it out; but at last he managed to ask:

"*Do* you know Julie Clarendon?" The name seemed to stick on his lips, and sounded much more like 'Clardon'. When Mannering didn't answer at once, he went on with an effort. "My information is that she greeted you with very great affection in Riston Street. Three of the Divisional officers were all of the opinion that you and she were close friends. Are you — sir?"

The 'sir' was obviously uttered with a great effort, proffered as a kind of olive branch in advance. "I have to ask but there's nothing personal in it," he seemed to say. And no one could have looked more directly, more challengingly.

"The first time I met her was at Quinns, this morning," Mannering stated with quiet emphasis. "That was the first time I've seen or heard of Tom Forrester, too. He wanted me to sponsor him, believing that patrons of the arts owe him a living. So far as I'm concerned the whole affair started from there." After a brief pause, without comment from Willison, he went on: "Ex-Superintendent Bristow now manages Quinns, as you no doubt know."

"I do," admitted Willison.

"He prepares a report on everything of interest which happens at Quinns," Mannering explained. "He'll have one on today's visitors by tomorrow afternoon. You are welcome to a copy."

"Thank you, Mr. Mannering," Willison said formally.

Mannering nodded, smiled, and turned away. When he looked into the bedroom Lorna was dressed in a tweed suit and wearing a wide-brimmed hat; obviously it had done her good to have to change. Her eyes were bright, too, and she looked at her best.

"Ravishing," he declared. "All ready?"

"Yes. Are you going to change? I've packed an overnight case for us both," Lorna added.

"Then I'll go just as I am," said Mannering.

Soon a police officer was standing aside at the door for them; the body was still in the flat. Seven or eight men were busy about the flat, so Willison was doing the most thorough job possible. A policeman in uniform was at the lift; another at the lift entrance on the street level hall; two more outside the house, where at least a dozen reporters and photographers waited.

"Sorry, darling," Mannering said. "This won't take long." He answered questions as they were flung at him, posed for photographers with Lorna, and then took the wheel of his station wagon, parked close by, and drove off. There was not much traffic, and it took only ten minutes for them to reach Eton Square. Here, six adjoining houses had been converted to a residential club fifty years ago, and Mannering had been a member for over half of that period.

It was like stepping into yesterday.

The doorman was more like a footman, the furniture was more suited to a home than to a club, there was an atmosphere of the Eighteenth Century, with paintings by English, Dutch and French masters, and furniture of the period. Their room had a huge bathroom leading off, and also an alcove where, if they preferred, they could prepare breakfast or any light meal. A maid was on floor duty, and she was unpacking when they left for the restaurant on the ground floor, a room of warmth and comfort which seemed to shut out much of the day.

They ate, leisurely, and talked desultorily about what had happened.

Lorna looked tired again when they were in the lounge, a club lounge more than one of a hotel, drinking coffee.

"John," she said, "just one question."

"Yes, my love?"

"Do you know more than you've told me?"

He smiled with amused understanding.

"No, darling," he answered. "There are some details

about what happened at Quinns and at Fulham but no dark secrets. I hadn't heard of the Fioras turning up again until the Yard asked to borrow Bristow to examine some pieces believed to be from the collection. I'd never heard of Julie or her Thomas, as I've just told Willison. I don't know what this is all about, but —" he hesitated, and looked intently at her : "but I'm going to have to help to find out."

"Must you?" she asked, almost hopelessly.

"Yes."

"Why?"

"Apart from what happened to you and the fact that someone tried to hang or choke the life out of me," Mannering replied quietly, "it seems possible that I may well be taken for a ride. It also seems probable that the police as well as the man who attacked you had been tipped off to believe that I have the Fioras. I want to find out why," Mannering finished simply. "Even you wouldn't want to stop me, would you?"

Lorna actually laughed.

"If I thought there was half-a-chance I would," she said. "But there isn't." There was comprehension in her expression as she went on : "So that's what Willison wanted us away for : he's searching the flat for the Fioras !"

"Precisely !"

"Why on earth did you let him?"

"Because he can't possibly find them," Mannering answered, "and hopefully that will be good for his soul and for his future attitude towards me." Before Lorna could interrupt, he went on : "I don't know what to make of him yet, but I'm going to have to make up my mind and learn from experience. If he's the man who's going to step into Bristow's shoes, I'll often be in touch with him. That's almost inevitable. And I didn't want to start off on the wrong foot. So once I realised what he was after, I decided to co-operate fully."

"He'll never be like Bristow," Lorna said, frowning.

"Bill and I were at each other's throats for years," Mannering reminded her. "You didn't exactly love him in the early days, either. You can't have forgotten."

"He was never a cold fish like Willison," Lorna replied, and stifled a yawn which came unbidden. "No doubt you'll handle him in your own inimitable way, dear. I wish it had never happened, but I do know that you won't rest until you've discovered what it's all about." She pushed her chair back, and Mannering stood up quickly and drew it away from her.

It wasn't until she was in bed, watching Mannering as he put on his pyjamas, that she said sleepily: "I hope he doesn't turn the place upside down."

"I think you'll find that he's a very neat and tidy man," Mannering replied, and slipped into bed.

Chief Inspector Leonard Willison was, in fact, an immaculate man in personal habits and in his work. Those who had carried out investigations with him before knew this. They all regarded Willison as a cold fish but they respected him, and they knew better than to be slapdash or untidy. So the search of the flat in Green Street, while thorough, left every room, every drawer and every cupboard exactly as Lorna herself had left it. Yet even carpets were taken up and floorboards checked for any which had been lifted recently, and might conceal a hiding place.

He found nothing at all to suggest that Mannering had lied, everything to indicate that things had happened as Mannering and his handsome wife had said. The bullet in the panelling had come from the gun which had only the dead man's fingerprints on it, an old-fashioned .30 Webley.

It was nearly two o'clock when the search was finished, and the men were all obviously tired. The body had been removed, the hall and the outside of the door checked for fingerprints and other clues; even the newspapermen had been given a statement and except for one man, on the *National Echo*, they had gone home. While his men were packing up, Willison sat on the arm of a big Regency chair,

Mannering's favourite, and for the first time, began to turn the pages of one of the press cuttings books.

On the instant, he felt a shock of surprise: a kind of intuition.

For this book had press cuttings which went back well over twenty years, and mostly concerned the exploits of the Baron.

Willison began to read, closely; fascinated, enthralled.

He read about the Baron, soubriquet for a Raffles-like thief who had a constant duel with then Chief Inspector William Bristow. His men were packed up and ready to go but none made a move to disturb him, for they saw from the intensity with which he read that he was absorbed.

What they could not see was into his mind: to the fact that his heart was beginning to pound with a new kind of excitement, fed by the growing conviction that the cracksman known as the Baron had been John Mannering, whom some called the Baron to this day.

But that original Baron had never been caught, never been punished for his crimes.

10

Dedicated Detective

WILLISON WAS A DEDICATED detective.

He was not simply a policeman; not simply a dedicated policeman. In fact, the rights and wrongs of a situation did not greatly affect him. He knew the law and applied it dispassionately but he felt no particular sense of triumph or pleasure because a man or woman had been caught and found guilty. His concern was with the problem; the untangling of the threads and the final solution. That was why he had been so anxious to search the Mannerings' apartment. It had not seriously occurred to him that John Mannering might be involved in the buying and selling of stolen jewels, only that he might have become involved as a third party — a kind of referee.

Now, Willison saw two different possibilities: that Mannering, once a thief as the cuttings seemed to show, might still be one; and that if in fact Mannering had never been caught then he, Willison, might have a chance to unravel mysteries buried deep in the past: mysteries with clues lost in the old files of Scotland Yard, or here in Mannering's flat, or in his and in his wife's mind.

Willison felt as if he were on the threshold of great new adventures in detection: a whole new world of possibilities.

He closed the book, held it on his lap for a few moments, heard someone cough, looked up and saw Detective Sergeant Joslin, from Fulham, in the doorway.

"We're all set now, sir, if you are," he said with a brightness which his over-tired eyes belied.

Willison looked at him blankly and for what seemed a long time; then he seemed to snap out of whatever was pre-occupying him. He put the heavy book back on the pile, nodded, took a quick but exhaustive tour of the flat to satisfy himself that everything had been left in apple-pie order, then gave instructions for the men to go, except for two, on night duty, who would guard the flat. For if the dead man had believed that the stolen Fiora Collection was at Mannering's flat, others might know or suspect this.

He reached his own small, bachelor flat in Victoria, a stone's throw from the Yard, at half-past three, set his alarm for half-past eight, and made himself a milk drink before getting into bed. He felt as nearly contented as he could be, and was asleep within a very few minutes.

Everyone involved was asleep, too.

Lorna was stirring when Mannering came out of the bathroom at nine o'clock that morning, and an electric kettle in the kitchen was already steaming. He made tea, took it across to her, was satisfied that she looked rested, and displayed the minor scars of his own battles : bruises on both knees and about his neck, where the noose had tugged, several grazes, including one on his left cheek-bone and several on his fingers, and a slightly puffy right ankle.

"But I feel as good as new," Mannering insisted, and drank tea, and surveyed Lorna. "How is your feminine commonsense this morning?" he asked.

"What about, in particular," Lorna asked suspiciously.

"Staying here and recuperating," Mannering suggested.

"Are *you* going to recuperate?"

"I'm going to take it easy," Mannering assured her. "Supposing you stay in bed until lunch, and I join you here."

Lorna pursed her lips, hesitated, and then leaned back on thick down-filled pillows.

"It sounds a lovely idea," she declared. "But I shall want a copy of every morning newspaper. Then I shall find out what the public know about my husband that I don't know."

"I'll see you get them all, uncensored," promised Mannering.

He sent for the newspapers, made coffee and toast when he was dressed and ready to go, saw banner headlines and photographs of Forrester, Julie and himself. It was in the *Daily Mail* that there was a full page picture of Julie rushing towards him, with her arms outstretched; it was as nearly perfect as a newspaper photograph could be. Taken broadside-on to them both, it showed the expression on Julie's face : longing, eagerness, hope. He, Mannering, saw it before Lorna, and when she had scanned the paper she was reading, he handed the *Mail* to her opened at the photograph.

Lorna studied it closely, and then looked at him, smiling, affectionate.

"She's very pretty, darling."

"That I know," said Mannering. "I also thought she was good."

"Do you have any reason to doubt it?"

"If she's trying to imply that we are old friends — yes, I have very much doubt."

"How can you find out?" Lorna asked.

"By seeing more of her," Mannering answered, leaning forward and stroking her cheek. "In spite of the misinterpretation some people may put on that, too."

"*I* won't, darling," Lorna almost cooed.

He looked at her for what seemed a long time, and then replied :

"I'm quite sure you won't, my darling. But Willison might, and one or more of the newspapers may. I am probably going to be presented to the eager world as a gay Lothario."

"Oh, I don't doubt that for a moment," Lorna said.

She was still smiling.

The smile began to fade as his expression changed and his eyes gleamed wickedly; there was obviously something on his mind which she didn't understand. They were like that for some time, Lorna against the pillows, Mannering sitting on the side of her bed. At last, she stirred.

"What's going on in that Machiavellian mind of yours?" she demanded.

"I was thinking you were a beautiful woman."

"Thank you, kind sir."

"And a very clever artist."

"Such compliments," she said, half mockingly; and then her eyes widened. "John!"

"So your mind is as Machiavellian as mine," observed Mannering.

"You mean, I should find out what I can about Forrester."

"It would be a compassionate act from a famous professional to a zestful amateur," Mannering remarked, and then he covered her hand with his. "Darling, I don't know what I'm talking about. It's too dangerous."

Thoughtfully, Lorna replied : "Well, it's dangerous whether I know him or not. I *could* look at his paintings."

"Will you?"

"And isn't he a *very* attractive man?"

"So far as hippies can be."

"Are you sure he's a hippy?" demanded Lorna.

"No," Mannering answered. "I'm not really sure about anything that young man does or says, but I think you might help to find out whether he is an artist at heart or whether he's putting on an act."

"To fool you?"

"Among others, probably," Mannering replied. He sat silent for a long time, before going on : "I can't really see any urgent danger in it, but if you went along with Bristow —"

"Now how could I hope to find out what is in a passionate young man's mind if I take along a man old enough to be my father?" Lorna asked, her eyes laughing at him.

After a long pause, Mannering said : "I'm not at all sure I should have suggested this. Promise me one thing."

"What thing?"

"If you won't take Bristow, at least tell him or me or someone at the shop you're going to Fulham," pleaded Mannering.

"Oh, I'll promise that," Lorna said. She lay back on the pillows, looking rather like a woman painted by Botticelli, and smiled at him as she peered at him through her dark, sweeping lashes. "There's one other thing."

"Tell me," Mannering urged.

"I might have thought of this by myself, you know."

Keeping a straight face, Mannering retorted: "I simply don't believe you're as devious as all that."

Lorna drew in a deep breath, changed from laughter to a glare, and actually shook a fist at him.

"You devil! You expected me to come round to the idea, and got in first so that I couldn't go alone without letting someone know. You *devil*! I have a good mind to go without saying a word to a soul!"

He took the clenched fist between his two hands, squeezed, and asked in a pleading voice: "Don't, my darling. Whatever you do, don't do that."

When he left the room he felt quite sure that she would go to Fulham during the day, but not without letting someone at Quinns know. He himself was open-minded about what he would do: whether he should first go to see Julie or wait for her to come to him again. He drove to a car park just behind Hart Row and was actually opening the door of Quinns when he remembered promising to go and see Julie at eleven o'clock the previous night. Immediately, he was angry with himself, but that eased when he realised how much had happened after the promise.

Rupert Smith was talking to an extravagantly-dressed American woman about some early Roman vases in a cabinet near the window. Armitage was sitting with a Japanese at a desk with an illustrated folio open, the beautiful pictures being examined under a strong light. Bristow appeared from behind the partition, as spruce as always in light grey.

"Good morning, Bill!"

"Good morning," Bristow said. "I thought you would be sleeping it off."

"Lorna is," Mannering replied.

"So half the family has some sense," Bristow retorted, examining Mannering closely. "Are you as all right as you look?"

"I think so," Mannering answered cautiously, and unlocked the door of his office; only on rare occasions, emergencies, did anyone go into the office when he was not on the premises. "Come in." As he sat down, beneath a portrait of a cavalier who looked so like him it was uncanny, he went on : "Did you have any luck?"

"Not a great deal," Bristow answered. "I know more about Julie Clarendon now. She is the daughter of a Church of England clergyman, a vicar of a church in Devonshire, and apparently her parents were very upset when she decided to come to London on her own. They know she is living with Forrester but it's not discussed between them. She goes home for an occasional weekend, but things are always pretty tense."

"How on earth did you learn all this?" demanded Mannering.

"I telephoned the Exeter police and they told me of a cousin who lives in Hampshire. At one time Julie was reported missing and they made some inquiries and found it was wilful missing. I went to see her last night, and she talked freely."

"Once a policeman always a policeman," Mannering said appreciatively. "And Forrester?"

"I haven't got so much about him," Bristow had to confess. "Julie's cousin says she thinks he's from a Midlands family and went to one of the minor public schools, then an art school in the Midlands, later to one at Chelsea. I don't yet know anything about his family but I've a few inquiries in process."

"I'll bet you have!" exclaimed Mannering. He pushed his chair back and looked up, head on one side, remembering how long he had known this man and how much they had come to like each other and work together. Since Bristow had left the Force and come to work here. "Bill — what do you know about the Fioras?"

"As much as the police tell me they know," answered Bristow. "There was a burglary at Sir Gordon Sangster's home last Thursday, and some jewellery was stolen. The police discovered the fence, who had the lot — including some Fiora pieces. When they went to see Sangster they discovered him literally at death's door; he'd had a severe heart attack — last Wednesday. Nothing's been said in the newspapers about the burglary, and the Yard is glad to help keep it quiet, so that they can investigate without being chased all the time by the Press."

Bristow paused long enough for Mannering to say : "And there's no trace of the rest of the collection? How much has been recovered?"

"Three pieces out of fifty-one," answered Bristow. "There are two theories, John. First, that the whole collection was taken and broken up, the thief learning how hot they were when the fence was questioned — so, he dumped them somewhere. Or else that a few pieces had been brought from some secret strong room at Sangster's house and stolen with family jewels. Sangster's only son, who lives at the London house with his wife, hasn't been questioned about any secret hiding-place yet. His concern appears to be only for his father."

Bristow stopped, shifted his position, and put a cigarette to his lips; it was very white against the dark nicotine of his clipped moustache. Abruptly, he asked : "Have they been offered to you?"

"No," replied Mannering, and went on in a deceptively casual voice : "But someone has told the police as well as the man who was killed at my flat that I have them."

"Who the hell would say that?" exclaimed Bristow.

"That's one of the urgent things to find out," Mannering replied, drily. They fell quiet for a while, studying each other. There were no sounds except that of distant voices and, suddenly, the opening and closing of the shop door. At last Mannering went on : "Have you heard how Forrester and the girl are this morning?"

"The girl's typing over at Number 20 Riston Street," answered Bristow. "Forrester is up and about, with a very stiff neck, but he's painting." Bristow smiled fleetingly : "I still have my friends at the Yard."

"We'll never need them more," Mannering said warmly. "Well! Let's look at the post."

Bristow went to fetch the morning's letters from his place at the bench behind the partition. There was very little beyond routine inquiries, and nothing that needed urgent attention. Mannering told Bristow that Lorna was likely to get in touch with Tom Forrester, but before Bristow could register either approval or disapproval, the telephone bell rang. Mannering picked up the receiver, and announced : "John Mannering." After a pause, he went on : "Yes, he's with me," and handed the receiver to Bristow, who took it as he sat on a corner of the desk.

"Yes ... Yes ... Oh, hallo, Joe." 'Joe' might be anyone as far as Mannering was concerned, and he went on making notes on the letters, giving instructions as to what was to be done. He heard what Bristow said, even sensed a sharpening in his inflection, but it wasn't until the other had put down the receiver and was looking down at him that he sensed anything was wrong.

"What is it?" he demanded sharply.

"That was Joe Pascall," Bristow stated, naming one of the senior members of the Criminal Investigation Department. "And he feels like sticking his neck out for both you and me." Bristow looked at once angry and bleak, and his hand was tight on the telephone, which he hadn't let go. "Apparently Willison has spent two hours this morning going over my old files, or rather the files of the cases I investigated back in the days when you and I weren't exactly friends. He's trying to dig up the past, John. Have you the faintest idea why he should?"

"No," said Mannering, very slowly. "No, I hoped he —"

he broke off, and understanding dawned. "Unless he examined my press cuttings book last night. I showed him how the settle safe works, and it did cross my mind that he might wonder what was in the books, but there was nothing I could do about it : the vital thing was to make sure he was convinced the Fioras were not at the flat."

II

Past and Present

THE YEARS ROLLED BACK for these two men.

In this same room they had stood as bitter adversaries, Bristow as hostile as ever Willison could be, positive that Mannering was the Baron but having no proof at all. Now they were on the same side but in virtually the same situation, and for a few moments both were very tense. It was Mannering who relaxed first, leaning back in his chair and beginning to smile.

"After all, the cuttings prove nothing, Bill."

"They prove you've been so interested in the Baron that you have prepared press cuttings books which are works of art in themselves, and you keep them in the safest place you know," retorted Bristow. "John, it's no use blinking at facts. The past has come up and hit you in the face when you least want it. Willison hasn't proof about your association with past crimes, any more than I ever had, but this could influence any way he behaves. And it could make him feel sure you have the Fioras."

"That the leopard hasn't changed his spots," murmured Mannering, a glint in his eyes.

"This isn't remotely funny," Bristow rebuked.

Mannering chuckled.

"Oh, I don't know, Bill. It has its humours. Even the Fioras have come right out of the past and slapped me. I was wondering last night what Willison would have thought had he known that twenty years ago I had them in that settle!"

"He would probably have clapped the handcuffs on you." Bristow still sounded sharp, but his tension was easing. "Don't make any mistake, though; this gives us new problems, John. I'm not going to try to probe into the past, but I'm very interested in the present. If you haven't got the Fiora Collection, have you the faintest idea where they are?"

"No one trusts me, not my closest friend nor even my wife," Mannering remarked sadly. He looked very straightly into Bristow's eyes. "No, Bill. I know only what you and the police have told me, and that a man now dead thought I had them."

Bristow's gaze was equally direct.

"You're wrong," he said. "I believe you."

"Do you, Bill?" asked Mannering, and there was a steely tone in the lightness of his voice. "What would you do if I said I had them?"

Bristow did not answer at first; nor did he shift his gaze. At last, he said : "You haven't got them, so what does it matter?"

"I think it matters a great deal," Mannering insisted.

Suddenly he was in conflict with Bristow, and the conflict had arisen out of the situation which spanned the years. It took him back to the days when Bristow had challenged him in much the way he had just now, but this was very different. He reminded himself how different. Then it had been war between them; now Bristow was no longer a policeman, and was in Mannering's employ. In the few months since this transition had begun they had worked together without conflict of any kind. Now, they were watching each other warily; more like adversaries than partners.

Bristow broke the silence at last.

"How does it matter, John?"

"What would you do?" asked Mannering.

"I would want to know how they had come into your possession," Bristow replied. He smiled faintly but his lips were taut. He hadn't yet lit the cigarette but was rolling it between his fingers. "Unless I knew differently, I would assume you had a very good reason for holding them."

"Unless you knew differently," Mannering echoed.

"Yes, John." Bristow pushed his chair back, as if suddenly needing more room to breathe. Looking down on him was Lorna's smiling cavalier, showing the dash and the daring of the man she loved; behind him was the winged armchair with its fine tapestry covering, protecting the entrance to the strong room which ran deep beneath the floor. "John," he went on, awkwardly, "you must know that if —" he gulped. "If you —" he broke off again.

"Had reverted to the habits of my remote past," Mannering murmured.

"Er — yes. You *must* know that I would do anything, absolutely everything to help you if you were being pushed into a corner because you were trying to help someone else. I never have felt that the law was absolutely rigid, it can and should be bent. But if you felt it necessary to lie about having the Fioras or any other stolen goods, then what could I think except that you were back to the old tricks?" When Mannering didn't answer, just looked at him intently, he actually turned dark red as he burst out : "It would mean you couldn't trust me. If you couldn't trust me it would be because you were deliberately outside the law." His voice grew harsher and the flush began to fade. "And if you placed yourself deliberately against the law, I couldn't work with you."

"Just as a leopard cannot change his spots, once a policeman always a policeman," Mannering said lightly. Now his smile made him the living image of the portrait above his head. "Of course you couldn't work with me if I didn't trust you. I — ah — couldn't work with you if you didn't trust me, either !" He picked up a book of matches, struck one, and held the flame towards Bristow, who put the cigarette slowly to his lips; he was scarlet again.

"Er — no, I suppose not," he muttered, and drew the flame on to the tip of the cigarette. "Of course you couldn't. It would be an impossible situation." He choked on the smoke, and it was several seconds before he could go on : "Mutual trust is vital if we're going to work together. Thanks. Er — who *would* want to lie to the police and to the dead man, about you having the Fioras?"

"Presumably, whoever has them and wants the police looking in the wrong place," Mannering responded. "Did you find out the name of the man who raided the flat?"

"Walker," answered Bristow promptly. "Jacob Walker. He had a record for breaking and entering, and he's an electrical engineer by trade, so he might have been a specialist on breaking safes open and forcing locks and sidetracking burglar alarms. Willison is checking, of course, the division's sending men to Walker's home."

"Was he married?"

"Wife and two kids," Bristow replied. "Twin girls of three."

There was the sadness and the tragedy : a woman suddenly widowed, children branded by their father's roguery, and likely to live for ever haunted by the knowledge that he had been murdered, and that he had himself been ready to kill. The silence touched both men with the same kind of disquiet, and lasted for a long time before Mannering broke it.

"Do what you can to find Walker's accomplices, will you? And keep your ear to the ground. Oh — I promised Willison a copy of the report I was sure you'd have made about the visit from the Forresters."

"I've a spare copy," Bristow said, with a sudden grin. He pushed his chair back, looked up at the portrait, and then shook his head slowly from side to side. "She's a remarkable woman," he said. "Nearly as remarkable as you are a man !"

He went out, carrying a sheaf of letters, and Mannering moved round the front of the desk and looked up at the portrait. But he didn't really see himself : he saw Lorna, an intent Lorna, and he wondered what was going on in her mind. Then he was called into the shop where the American woman had reached the stage of making an offer for the

Roman vases and Rupert Smith could not handle such an offer by himself. The largest was worth at least eleven hundred pounds, Mannering knew; it was made in the first century B.C., probably by an Etruscan potter, and such work was very rare indeed. The woman offered seven hundred and fifty pounds, most charmingly.

"I'm sorry," Mannering said. "It's priced at twelve fifty, and I can't come so far down."

"Oh, what a pity," she said. "But even though I can't afford so much, I *have* had the pleasure of speaking to the renowned John Mannering. And a real pleasure it is." Her blue eyes twinkled.

As he saw her out he wondered whether she had really come to buy, or simply to see him and spend a little time among the treasures she no doubt loved. The telephone bell rang on its muted note, and as he reached his office Armitage said:

"Mrs. Mannering, sir."

"Thanks." Mannering took the receiver. "Excuse me. Hallo, darling, how are you?"

"Too restless to stay in bed," Lorna told him, without preamble. "I'm going to Fulham, pet!" And she rang off even before he could tell her that Julie was at Number 20, Riston Street. He picked up the telephone, dialled Scotland Yard, and asked for Willison. After only a few moments came Willison's unmistakable voice, sounding almost reedy on the telephone. "This is Willison."

"Good morning, Chief Inspector," Mannering said.

"Who —" Willison began, and then stopped abruptly. "Good morning, Mr. Mannering."

"Have you got your man yet?" asked Mannering.

"No, sir."

"I hope you get him soon. You have men in Riston Street, Fulham, haven't you?"

"Yes, for the time being. May I ask why you're interested?"

"My wife tells me she's going to see Forrester's paintings

this morning," answered Mannering. "I wouldn't like to think she would be alone in case an attacker is lurking."

"I'll make sure she isn't in danger," Willison promised. "Is that all, Mr. Mannering?"

"Unless you'd like to tell me whether you identified the dead man."

"He was a Jacob Walker," Willison answered without hesitation, "and he has a criminal record. Had you ever heard of him before?"

"No," Mannering replied; and then he asked with a chuckle in his voice: "Did you find anything of interest in your search last night?"

Willison caught his breath, but didn't answer immediately. Then for the first time a hint of laughter sounded in his voice:

"I found some very interesting things, indeed, Mr. Mannering. Thought-provoking things."

And he rang off.

Lorna Mannering had a bright red Elf, a mini-Riley, for running about London when on her own, and she drove it that morning. She was between sittings, and had deliberately given herself a few days off; one could work too hard, and she found it difficult to say 'no' to the constant stream of people who wanted her to paint them. She turned the car into Riston Street a little before twelve o'clock, seeing it exactly as John had described it, and when she got out she looked up and down, appraising the street as a subject. Very Victorian and once very poor, it was now going through a period of prosperity, and the bright paint in many colours gave it a baroque kind of appearance which wasn't unpleasing.

A policeman stood outside Number 17.

"Good morning, Miss."

A nice little flattery, Lorna thought appreciatively, and gave her brightest smile.

"Good morning. Do you know if Mr. Forrester is in?"

"He is, miss, yes." The policeman had a nice skin, nice

eyes, a badly broken nose. "May I ask what your business is?"

"I am an artist, too."

"You *are* Mrs. Mannering, then!"

"Yes," Lorna replied, faintly flattered at being recognised.

"Very glad to meet you," said the policeman. "It was a pleasure to meet Mr. Mannering yesterday, too." Concern shadowed bright grey eyes. "He's all right, I hope."

"He's fine, thank you," Lorna assured him, and turned to the house.

She was aware of a dried-up face and spiky grey hair at the window; this would be the old man John had told her about. She pretended not to notice him, and rang the top doorbell. There was no answer. She rang again, and when there was still no answer the policeman spoke from the pavement.

"I know he's in."

On his words, the door opened, and the bent old man appeared, peering up at her. "Morning," he said, in his wheezy voice, and stood aside. "Never answers the bell, he doesn't, thinks I'm his lackey, he does." He pressed back against the wall as Lorna entered, and at the same time a pair of feet in vivid red socks appeared at the head of the narrow stairs, and a man called in a loud, exasperated voice :

"Who the hell's that? If I worked in a factory you wouldn't come barging in —"

He broke off, with a lame : "Oh," on sight of Lorna.

"Good morning," Lorna said sweetly. "I now know exactly what my husband meant when he described you."

Tom Forrester did not speak again but came quickly down the stairs, blue jeans above the red socks, vivid yellow shirt stuffed in at tiny waist; the jeans needed no belt. His hair was tousled, his face particularly handsome in the shadowy hall. He looked at her very intently as he reached the bottom tread, and in a different, a pleasing tone of voice, he asked :

"Mrs. Mannering?"

"Yes."

"It is *very* good of you to come."

"I am glad to," she said.

He made no reference to his rudeness but made way for her to pass and followed closely up the stairs, saying : "Turn left and go straight on." She did so but could not fail to notice the bathroom or see the wall-pictures; and she shuddered involuntarily because she could imagine the noose, hanging down. She hoped Forrester did not notice the shudder. The door of the front room was open and she stepped inside.

Although there was an air of disarray and colour-clashes, she was quick to see that both scheme and untidiness were considered. In its vivid way, it was a beautiful room; the room of an artist. In one corner was a huge plastic bubble chair in vivid blue, and on the divan bed and the floor were many scatter cushions as well as cushions large enough to sit on. She went towards the bubble chair as Forrester said :

"Do sit down." And when she was sitting, he gave a most charming smile. "Do you approve of the décor?"

"I don't think approval is the point," she replied. "I certainly like it."

"Thank you." When she simply smiled back, he went on : "Does this mean that your husband liked what he saw well enough to want a second opinion?"

"He told me there were some indications of an original mind," Lorna replied.

"It was very clever of him to notice, in view of what happened," Forrester said, wryly. "Did he — may I get you some coffee?"

"No thank you. I had a very late breakfast."

"So did I," confessed Forrester. "Did your husband tell you where most of my paintings are?"

"In the loo and in the attic with some in the kitchen," Lorna said. "I am very agile, Mr. Forrester."

He stood looking down at her, and she was puzzled and surprised at the change in his manner and the way he appraised her. He was frowning, and the lines between his

eyes and across his forehead became deep grooves. These
made him more striking to look at, and his eyes were vivid
blue and bright. He seemed older than John had suggested :
in the late twenties, not twenty-three or four. He stood
looking down at her for so long that it became embarrass-
ing, but she did not feel inclined to turn away.

He seemed to grow larger, and to draw closer, although
he did not move.

She could not prevent her heart from thumping with an
emotion she couldn't identify, except as fear, yet 'fear'
wasn't really the word. She was very much aware of him as
a man, and had no doubt at all that he meant her
to be.

Then his lips parted and he began to speak, slowly, very
deliberately.

"You are a most beautiful woman, Mrs. Mannering. And
a most desirable woman. Does your husband tell you that
often enough?"

12

Artist's Licence

As FORRESTER FINISHED, HE smiled.

There was nothing predatory about it, but there was
daring with a hint of danger. She did not think she had
ever met a more masculine man; one who by his very pose
and manner could make her aware not only of him, but
of herself. Had John told her that he would behave like
this she would have said laughingly: "I can look after
myself, darling," and she would have felt quite sure.

And of course she was sure : wasn't she?

It was uncanny that he could loom so large and near
without moving. Or was he moving? Had he drawn a little
closer? Whether he had or not, her heart was thumping
louder and the sense of fear was greater, her breathing was
much more shallow, each breath coming through slightly
parted lips. She wanted to make some casual or commonplace comment, to pretend that she was not aware of this —
this magnetism in him, but if she spoke while her heart was
thumping so it would be gaspingly, and that would be fatal.

Fatal? What on earth was the matter with her?

Now he moved, closer, and held out his hands.

"I can see he doesn't," he said. "Too many men take
their wives too much for granted. Don't they?"

She didn't put out her hands although the impulse to do
so was nearly irresistible. She could not move further back
in the chair which seemed to close about her, holding her
back, her waist, her thighs : hugging her. She sensed, she

knew, that if she yielded even so far as putting out her hands, she would be lost.

Nonsense!

But it wasn't nonsense. This was real. She was sitting in the corner in a chair from which she couldn't rise without holding or pressing against something to help herself up, and only this man's hands were within reach. And they were drawing closer, long, pale, strong-looking hands.

"Lorna," he said, "you are mature enough to know better."

At last, she could control her voice well enough to answer: "Better than what?" The words came out quite clearly but perhaps with a shade of vehemence.

"You know perfectly well what I mean," he said.

"No," she denied. "I don't."

But her heart was now thumping furiously and she was breathing with greater difficulty even than before.

"You do," he insisted. "You are a very beautiful and desirable woman and I am a handsome, strong and virile man. We have been thrown together by chance and we have an opportunity to make love. Two perfect human beings with a perfect opportunity. And —" he moved again and rested his hands on her elbows. She could feel his strength, and sense the urgency of his desire. "No one need know," he went on. "If you live in a comfortable convention-cluttered world, no one need know. I promise you."

The pressure of his hands grew stronger, and he began to lift her. She was surprised how easy it was for him. And he was utterly serious. He had such confidence in his mastery that it did not seem to occur to him that she would not be compliant. He was smiling more broadly, and the glint of his teeth against the harp-shaped lips made him very like John. John. The unbelievable thing was that she was so acutely aware of his overwhelming masculinity; there had been a time when she would have yielded as she had, all those years ago, to John.

But she had been in love with John.

This wasn't *love*.

This wasn't even conscious attraction; only awareness. It was as if this man had cast a spell over her.

"Lorna," he said, his lips very close to her cheek. "Don't resist. You'll only spoil things if you resist. You are quite beautiful. Adorable. Utterly desirable."

He drew his hands up along her arms towards her shoulders, and tilted her head back, so as to kiss. She did not know quite what it was that clicked in her mind; a kind of reflex action as strong as the attraction of this man. She spoke again and much more softly, whispering, almost as if she were answering seduction with seduction.

"You really are a most arrogant boy, you know."

He was so shocked that his hold on her loosened, and effortlessly she moved to one side, between him and the wall. He made a grab at her but she avoided his hands as if she was unaware of them, reached the end of the divan and, as he took a long stride towards her, went to the window and looked out into the street.

Forrester came very close to her but all her fear had gone and the half-formed temptation had vanished too; she was in complete control of herself. She peered further out, and saw the top of the policeman's helmet. A car passed, noisy but slow. She turned to look at Forrester, smiling quite freely.

"You may not believe it," she said "but I really did come to see your paintings."

Her eyes laughed at him.

She thought, this will help to find out what he's really like. If there's any humour in him, and any gallantry, it will show now. But if he were truly arrogant, if a repulse carried real injury to his pride, then he was worth no one's trouble, least of all John's.

Suddenly, he backed to the bed and dropped down on it, raising his hands palms outwards in a gesture of surrender. And whatever he was feeling, outwardly he began to laugh at her *congé*.

"I give in," he said. "You'll live to regret it, though."

"If I do, I can always come to you," she retorted lightly.

"As a supplicant? You? Not on your life!" He moved further back on the bed. "You wouldn't care to change your mind?"

"No, thank you."

"Ah, me. The old world has talons that hold you fast. The period of transition is hard. But if I can't persuade you, I *can* show you my etch — paintings."

"Please," she said.

"You will still look at them?"

"Didn't you say something about art for art's sake to my husband?"

"If I didn't I've no doubt I implied it," Forrester conceded. "So in spite of my outrageous behaviour you will look at my work?"

"Yes, of course," Lorna said. "I may not want to be compliant but I can be flattered that you should want me to be."

"The incredible Lorna Mannering," exclaimed Forrester, springing to his feet with startling agility. "Instead of crushing me with your refusal you make me feel both virtuous and virile; the virtue is not usually one of my moods, except of course in my work." He held out one hand and she placed hers in it lightly. "Come into my bathroom," he invited, his eyes gleaming, "and see the wondrous pictures on the loveliest loo in London." They reached the door and he spread out both arms to encompass walls and bath, pedestal and ceiling. "Observe! And the police obligingly supplied a loft ladder, on loan, so that access to the attic is no longer difficult or, for the beskirted, indelicate. There used to be just a chair which could turn into a ladder of sorts. The nimble had no trouble, as witness yesterday's intruder. Now while you're appraising the gems artistic here I will go up and make sure no one is skulking in the attic this morning."

He bowed from the waist and turned and mounted the ladder which rose at a sharp angle from floor to hatch. He moved so lightly that she hardly heard him. And after a few moments she became so absorbed in the painting, of succulent breasts and enticing nipples, and, all around, the mouths of babes open in eagerness to suckle. Then she went into the kitchen and spent perhaps ten minutes in there. He had taken the murals at Pompeii for his models, she felt sure, but the subject matter concerned her less than the texture of the painting, and its style. One word occurred to her : relaxed. It was more than competent and had a quality of communication which was rare.

When she went out, Forrester was sitting at the head of the ladder, his legs dangling; the bright red socks were obviously hand-knitted. He did not ask what opinion she had formed but sprang back, squatted, and helped her into the attic. There was more light than when Mannering had seen it, for cleverly concealed fluorescent lamps were switched on among the rafters, and here and there a floodlight, equally well-concealed, shone on a group of the small paintings. They were all faces; families of faces, of every size and shape and colour. John had told her of them and yet she had not even begun to understand the variety and the cleverness of the execution.

"Mrs. Man —" he began.

"Lorna," she interrupted.

"Thank you. For a square you *are* a pet! May I sketch you?"

"Now?"

"Please," he begged.

"If you really want to," she conceded.

"Oh, I do! There's a stool over here." He moved a leather or plastic seated stool close to a beam, and took her arm and drew her to the seat. "Just sit there and put your elbow on the rafter for comfort. And — keep still, won't you?"

She wondered how many hundreds of times she had said that to a sitter or a model.

He had placed her so that she could see him working and he put up an easel and placed a piece of hardboard on it, took a palette and a brush, which he held up as if he were using it to help him get her face in focus. Then he began;

and seemed to undergo a metamorphosis, much as John's —
remarkably like John's when he was concentrating on a
problem or examining some jewels which he hadn't seen
before. Everything else dropped away from John: and
everything but what he was doing seemed to fade from
Forrester's mind. He worked quickly and with a sure touch;
a professional's touch. Certainly he was no dilettante, but
then, the number of pictures in this flat proved that. Now
and again he looked across at her, his eyes quite brilliant,
his gaze so naked that he seemed to be stripping her of
make-up of every kind and was seeing her as she really
was.

She began to feel stiff and uncomfortable but did not
shift her position. She was aware of noises in the back
garden, of distant traffic, high-flying aircraft, a car horn.
She began to think of what had happened here yesterday
and what John had told her, and she knew why she had
really come and what questions she wanted to ask
Forrester. But his concentration was so great, so fierce, that
she kept silent; but she did not think she could keep still
much longer.

Then suddenly, he backed away and let his arms fall
by his side; and he seemed to let the breath out of his
body like the air hissing out of a punctured tyre.

"Like to see it?" he asked, flatly.

"May I?"

"As a special privilege. And if I can rely on you not
to comment."

She slid off the stool but didn't move towards him; his
manner was challenging again, the arrogance was back.

"Not even if I like it?"

"You would say you did whether you did or not. All
kind-hearted people do. And in any case you would only
form a quick impression, you would give me a reaction,
not an opinion. I distrust reactions."

"I may want to ask questions," Lorna said.

"I think that will be all right," he conceded.

She was startled : "Only *think*?"

"I don't remember having been asked intelligent questions about my painting," he said. "Certainly not just after I've finished a session. I am seldom watched, of course. Or scrutinised."

She moved across, without speaking. He was pale and there was a beading of sweat, a mass of tiny globules, on his forehead and upper lip. Tension? Reaction, once he had finished the sketch. She knew how quickly that could come after a period of concentration; how utterly exhausted one could feel. He moved aside to allow her to get in front of the easel, and he looked at the north light, as if anxious not to see her expression, but he couldn't keep his gaze averted and although she couldn't see them, the deep grooves were in his forehead and a network of crows' feet was at his eyes.

She looked at herself.

The astonishing, the unbelievable thing was that he had caught her likeness exactly as she had been twenty or twenty-five years ago. The freshness, the bloom. The eagerness which was born of innocence. The features might or might not be right, but the expression was : it was like looking at her long lost, beloved past.

She turned to look at him, and quickly he moved to the window. She shifted her position two or three times to see the painting from different angles. Soon, she crossed to the other paintings, so skilfully lit, and after a while, she asked :

"Do you always have models?"

"Whenever I can."

"These negroes," she pointed.

"Notting Hill or Hammersmith," he answered, "Or on the other side of Wandsworth Bridge Road. Sometimes I sketch. Usually I can keep the models in my mind's eye until I get back here. Then —" he broke off, wiping his forehead with a tiny ball of a paper handkerchief.

"Then you rush round here and get it on canvas or hardboard before the picture fades from the mind."

"So you know," he breathed. "You know."

"I can see how much you take out of yourself," she remarked gently.

"Very few can. No one can. Julie pretends to but only because I keep telling her so. She really wouldn't mind if I wiped my feet on her." When Lorna didn't comment, he went on : "I was pretty sure when I saw you in the hall. I was sure when I saw you sitting in the corner. You know what happens when one pours oneself into a creation. So you must experience it." He moved nearer, still wiping his forehead. "It's like — it's like the way tension builds and leads to an orgasm. Did you ever think of that similarity?"

"No," she answered.

"But you see what I mean?"

After a few moments, Lorna said quietly : "Yes. All your strength, all your nervous energy, everything in your body and your metabolism are concentrated on what you're painting, and nothing else matters." After a moment she repeated : "And nothing else matters."

He gave her a strange look, and said :

"Nothing else exists."

She thought : And it doesn't, with John and me. She thought again : And it doesn't when this man is painting.

"Tom," she said.

"Yes?"

"Is it always like this when you paint?"

"If it isn't, I paint over the picture and start afresh." He was much less exhausted now, and gave a fierce grin. "Mind you, some models arouse me to instant action more than others. As some women ! You did both, which is quite remarkable. And I'm glad you weren't —" he broke off, frowning, and then asked. "What was the word you used?"

"Compliant," she supplied.

"I'm glad you weren't, or all my energy would have been concentrated on you then and I'd still be exhausted now. We have something to show for this, not simply remembered pleasure." He gave a short bark of a laugh and let his hands fall on to her shoulders as he went on : "I'm breaking all my rules today. I'll break another one. Do you like this fantasy of you, or do you hate it? Do you think it's the real you beneath the make-up and the sophistication, the worldly experience and the wisdom — or do you think it's pallid and weak?" He stopped and held his breath, and then commanded: "Come on, tell me." And then suddenly his tone changed, the arrogance faded into humility, and he pleaded: "Please."

13

Opinion

THE QUESTION HAD BEEN inevitable, of course; there wasn't
an artist in the world who did not want to know what
others thought of his work, and longed for approval and
for praise. No one could be indifferent, and despite this
man's poise he was as eager and as vulnerable as any;
perhaps more, because he tried so hard to conceal it.

"Tom," Lorna said, "a sitter is no better judge of a
portrait than the painter, *I* like this. I'm astonished you did
such a finished picture so quickly, without a sketch or
drawing to base it on, and I'm not sure whether that's a
good thing or a bad. Do you always work so swiftly?"

"As I told you, if it's any good, yes," he answered. "You
— you like it?"

"Very much. I think John will, too. I'd like him to see it
without being prepared — reactions *can* be valuable."

Forrester laughed in a slightly embarrassed way.

"Touché," he said. "The —" he waved his arms about,
and mumbled a question she could guess rather than hear.
"The others?"

"You certainly have an original style which comes from
an original mind. I think you could become a fashion. I'd
need to see more range of work over a longer period before
saying whether I think you've even a touch of genius. But
whatever the galleries and the experts say, you are not wast-
ing your time and you are — as an artist!" she added with
a smile —"worth helping."

He stood very still before he said : "Thank you. Thank

you very much." And the humility was again quite unmistakable.

"And both my husband and I will try to help," Lorna went on. She stopped, and for once he seemed incapable of words, so she changed the subject completely, by asking : "Tom — why did someone try to kill you yesterday? And why did someone try to kill John?"

She put the questions very directly, as if she knew that he could answer if he would. And she had posed them when he was in a gentler mood, perhaps a mood in which to answer.

He stood more stiffly. His eyes narrowed and his lips tightened, until suddenly he said with harshness and antagonism in his voice :

"Nonsense. No one tried to kill me, I tried to kill myself. As for what happened to the great John Mannering, I neither know nor care. And if you gave me a lot of bull about my work in the hope of softening me up, you wasted your time. I don't need help. I should have listened to Julie and not gone to see your precious husband. You can take it from me I'll never go again."

He was flushed with anger and his eyes were feverishly bright. She realised even as he was talking that this was no time to try to persuade him that he was wrong, every comment about his work had been genuine although he thought she had been simply breaking down his resistance so that he would talk. Every moment she spent here now would be wasted, so she turned away and stepped to the top of the ladder supporting herself by holding a rafter, then started backwards down the stairs.

She was nearly at the foot when she realised that someone else was there, and she glanced round to see a man in a well-cut Edwardian suit of khaki colour, black, shiny hair, dark eyes bright with obvious admiration. She couldn't be sure, but she thought this was the neighbour, Clive Paget.

She wondered what he was doing here and why he had come in so quietly. She wondered how much he had heard of the conversation. And she wondered in the back of her

mind why Tom Forrester had denied that someone had
tried to murder him, preferring her to think that he had
tried to kill himself. She was beginning to feel a kind of
delayed shock after what had happened when she had
first arrived, and her legs were unsteady.

The man put out a hand to steady her as she reached
the floor. It was a firm, cool hand.

"Thank you," she said.

"My pleasure." He gave a bright smile and did not
hesitate to show his admiration but there was nothing over-
bold in his manner. "Is Tom — Mr. Forrester — coming
down, do you know?"

"I should doubt it," Lorna answered.

"I just nipped in for a quick word with him," said the
other man. "My name is Paget, Clive Paget. Er — will you
be staying?"

"No, I'm about to leave."

"Tell you what," replied Paget, leaning close and touching her arm lightly, "will you tell Mr. Mannering I'd like
a word with him some time soon? Thanks a lot." He moved
to the ladder and raised his voice. "Tom! Tom! I'm coming
up." He went nimbly up the ladder and Lorna saw his
shiny black shoes almost twinkling; it was hard to think of
anything more different from Forrester's red socks.

She went downstairs, still feeling a little breathless; she
seemed only now to be realising exactly what had happened
between her and Forrester; was only now beginning to recall the impact he had made, the way she had been so
vividly aware of his masculinity. She had a feeling that she
had only managed to save herself from a situation as com-
promising as one could be; that he had set out to seduce
her from the moment he had realised who she was.

Then, like a thunderclap, came another realisation : the
girl Julie might be attempting to seduce John!

"Good gracious!" Lorna exclaimed aloud.

She opened the door of the Elf, and at the same time
looked over the top of the car. A young woman was coming out of the door of a brightly painted house opposite

Number 17. She was fresh and attractive in a pale green blouse and a dark brown mini-skirt, and she had beautiful legs sheathed in flesh-coloured nylons. She did not glance across at Lorna, only up and down as if to make sure the road was clear, then hurried to Number 17 and went inside.

So now Forrester, Paget and the girl were together.

"I wonder what John would do in these circumstances," Lorna asked aloud and laughed. "I know what I'm going to do!"

She got into her car and drove off.

After a few minutes she felt a slight prickly sensation in her arms and legs, like incipient pins and needles. She began to shiver. A car, passing on the inside as she turned out of Wandsworth Bridge Road into New King's Road, made her jump so much that her heart began to hammer. She drove very carefully, telling herself that she must concentrate, after all it wasn't far to Green Street. Had she much further to go she would have pulled into a side street and parked until she felt calmer. This was delayed shock, of course. She had never known a man behave as Forrester, but that was far from the most significant factor; far more astonishing was her own response, the inner struggle she had been forced to make against the impulse to be 'compliant'.

She turned the wheel towards Green Street, and a car horn blared; a small pale blue car with a dark-haired man in it roared past, the man glaring. Very carefully she turned into the street and pulled up outside their house. A few people stood about, a tall policeman was in the doorway. With another sense of shock she realised that she had left from the Club that morning, and she shouldn't have come back here.

But she wanted rest; she needed some aspirins and some tea.

The policeman came towards her.

"Can I help you, Mrs. Mannering?"

"Yes, I think so. Is my flat free, yet?"

"Yes, madam. There's a sergeant and a detective officer upstairs, but they'll be through in a few minutes. I'm sure you can go up."

"Thank you," she said, as he opened the street door for her.

The sergeant and another man, whom she had seen last night, were about to close the lift door as she reached her landing, and the sergeant drew up.

"Good afternoon, Mrs. Mannering."

"I'm very glad you've finished," Lorna said.

"All except for one thing," the sergeant told her. "I hope it won't be an inconvenience but the Chief Inspector asked us to lock the study door — the room where the intruder spent most of his time."

"I should think it will be all right," Lorna said, dubiously.

The sergeant frowned as he looked at her. Her headache was worse and she sensed that she was pale; obviously he had noticed that. He turned into the hallway with her, and asked in his deep but unmistakably Cockney voice :

"Are you all right, ma'am?"

"I — I'm a little overtired," Lorna admitted. In fact she had suddenly recalled what had happened when she had last been here alone; remembered opening the door to the masked man with the gun. She had not really thought about that before; it seemed to have happened only a few minutes ago. "I'll make myself some coffee and lie down for a while."

"Let us make the coffee, please," the sergeant offered, and beckoned to the man outside. "You'll be much better if you sit down for half-an-hour before you do anything at all. Which room would you prefer?" She led the way into the bedroom, too tired to stand on any ceremony, and dropped into a chaise-longue.

"You're very kind."

"Glad to be of help, ma'am." The man was so broad and chubby and earnest and had the most attractive curly brown hair; and he had eyes more red than brown, and very shiny. Then suddenly he stiffened and alarm flared up in his eyes. "Nothing else is wrong, is it?" he asked. "Mr. Mannering's all right?"

"Oh yes," she said, touched by his obvious concern. "I'm just overtired and — well, I suddenly remembered how the man attacked me, and the fact that he was murdered here. Have you — have you caught the murderer?"

"Not yet, ma'am," the sergeant replied. "But we will, don't have any doubts about that. And there's no need at all for you to worry. There'll be a policeman on duty downstairs *and* in the hall up here. You're bound to be nervous for a little while, but you really needn't worry. Is Mr. Mannering coming?"

"He'll be in this evening," she answered. "He doesn't know I'm back here."

She sensed the man's flush of disapproval of John, but was too tired to worry about it. Soon the police officer came in with coffee on a tray with a lace mat he must have taken out of a kitchen drawer. There was coffee in a jug, cream, sugar, plain biscuits. He placed these on a table by her side, and stood back.

"I hope that's all right," he said diffidently.

"It looks wonderful! And if one of you could give me my handbag, I've some aspirins in it, I'll feel beautifully spoiled."

They fussed a little more before leaving, and there was a depressing finality about the closing of the outside door. She leaned back, shifting a cushion behind her head, and closed her eyes. A picture not of John, not of the policemen, but of Tom Forrester filled her mind's eye, and it did not go until she opened her eyes and poured out coffee. She put in plenty of sugar and a splash of cream, then drank slowly. It began to warm her almost at once. She had her feet up, and now unfastened the zipper at her waist; she had already kicked off her shoes.

What on earth was the matter with her?

She couldn't be frightened about last night. Not now. And she couldn't be interested in Forrester : that was ludicrous! But she *had* been virtually mesmerised. Or was it hypnotised? She could almost see his eyes and feel his hands. She remembered the effect of seeing the girl, too, and the way she had behaved with John. That picture in the *Mirror* had been quite remarkable; but then, what a picture she and Forrester would have made!

Suddenly, she exclaimed aloud: "That photograph!"

She had a sudden vision of the man who had run away from the house after Walker's death; saw him turn and look up, and recalled the expression on his face and the click of the camera. She sprang up, knocked the tray, saved it from toppling and hurried into the drawing room for the camera. She saw no sign of it, although the last time she had seen it it had been on a small table, after John had put it down. She picked up the telephone in the hall and dialled Quinns; John himself answered, in the deep voice which seemed to make the wire vibrate.

"John Mannering, of Quinns."

"John," Lorna said, almost in exclamation. "The camera!"

"What cam —" he began, and then suddenly laughed. "*The* camera! I brought it here and took the roll to a shop for developing. I've been promised it for this afternoon."

"Thank goodness for that," she exclaimed. "I thought you might have left it and the police had taken it. I'm back at the flat, darling. The study's still locked but everything else is clear, and I must say they left it immaculate."

"Good for Willison! Will you stay home now?" Mannering obviously wanted the answer to be 'Yes'.

"Oh, I think so."

"Then I'll call at the club for the things," he promised.

"Thank you, darling."

"Did you go to Riston Street?" John inquired.

"Yes," she answered. "I simply had to."

"How did you get on?"

It was on the tip of her tongue to say that Forrester had tried to do to her what Julie had apparently tried to do with him, but she stopped herself. In a swift succession of thoughts she told herself that once she started to explain

John would want to know more and more, and that if she
tried to explain Forrester's attitude and her own feeling,
John would never really understand. It was far better to
say nothing : she would soon forget and he would never
know.

So she answered : "John, I really think he's — he's good."

"Near genius?" asked John lightly.

"Very unusual anyway."

"So, worth helping?" he persisted.

"Decidedly," she answered. "But I doubt if he'll let
himself be helped now."

"You got that impression too?"

"Strongly," Lorna admitted.

"What did you do to affront him?" asked Mannering.

"I asked him why he pretended to have committed
suicide when in fact someone tried to murder him," said
Lorna. "His attitude changed so quickly he was hardly the
same man."

Mannering chuckled.

"I'm not really surprised," he said. "I never saw a man
whose mood can change so fast ! Did he answer?"

"He insisted that he attempted to commit suicide."

"Ah," said Mannering, softly. "Did he give you the
slightest hint why?"

"No," Lorna replied slowly, and after a few moments she
went on : "I think he meant to imply that he was doing it
as a martyr on the funeral pyre of art for art's sake, but I
can't say that he put it in those words. I may have dreamed
it up."

"Possibly," agreed Mannering. "But from what you saw
of him did he seem likely to try to take his own life?"

She could picture Forrester's brilliant eyes; his hand-
someness; she could feel his strength and believe in his
virility. He was as vivid a personality as she had ever
known, and had no doubt at all that he lived life to the
full and loved to the full, and would cling to it with all his
strength.

"No," she said, quietly. "I don't think he would for one moment."

"Nor do I," said Mannering. "So we have to find out who attempted to kill him, and why. And I've a feeling that you are much more likely to make him talk than I ever can."

14

Dilemma

LORNA HAD PLENTY OF time to ponder and even to brood over that remark, for Mannering rang off, after promising to get back as soon as he could, and in an almost fatherly way, urging her to have some rest.

To her surprise she actually dropped off to sleep for half-an-hour, and felt much better for it. She was able to consider the situation much more dispassionately, but still realised that his remark had thrust her into a dilemma.

When after getting home he said much the same thing — that she was much more likely to be able to make Forrester talk — her immediate reaction was still to think : *No*! I don't want another tête-a-tête with Tom Forrester. Yet John was almost certainly right; once Forrester had recovered from his annoyance, he was likely to talk more freely to her than to John. She was aware of the scrutiny of John's hazel brown eyes; became aware of the change from the quizzical to the puzzled in his expression. If she didn't answer soon he would know that something was the matter.

Was it? Or was she exaggerating?

Should she — oh, nonsense! She hadn't exaggerated Forrester's attitude or the strength of her own emotions.

Her silence had lasted too long, now, for her to avoid making some explanation, and it wouldn't be fair to wait until John asked what was troubling her. So she rested a hand on his arm, and said :

"He's a very headstrong man."

Mannering was still puzzled, and frowning as if bewildered, too.

"Yes, I know. But —" he widened his eyes in astonishment. "*That* kind of headstrong? He made a pass at you?"

"He was positively passionate," Lorna replied, her eyes suddenly brighter.

"But not, I trust, over-persistent?"

"No, darling," she said. "He took 'no' for an answer very nicely."

"But you're not sure that he always would, and don't want to try to make him talk," Mannering remarked. "Well, well!"

"I'm simply not sure that I want to use my womanly wiles on him," elaborated Lorna. "He might come to the conclusion that I was trying to make a deal with him."

"Ah," Mannering said, laughter sparkling in his eyes. But was there something as well as laughter? It was never really possible to be sure, and she wasn't sure now. "He's a strikingly handsome chap and I don't doubt that he finds a lot of women compliant." She was startled at his choice of word, but hoped that it didn't show in her eyes. "Darling, this has its fascinating aspects."

"*Has* it, sweetheart?"

"Yes, beloved. The pretty little Julie has decided to try to weaken my manly resistance, and handsome Tom is now exerting his masculine charms to involve you. *Can* it be that she's just a natural sex-kitten needing a strong pair of arms — in addition to the pair she has already! — and that he is simply knocked sideways by one of the loveliest women he's ever met? Or —"

Lorna bobbed a mock curtsey.

"Thank you, kind sir!"

"The truth will stand for ever! Or have they put their heads together and created some other, combined motive? Julie planning to seduce me; Thomas trying to seduce you. I wonder what they're really after." He mused for a few moments before going on in a brisker voice. "I know what we'll do! I'll tackle Forrester while you tackle Julie!"

"What on earth makes you think that will get results?" asked Lorna.

"If it doesn't, we can think again," Mannering replied; the idea obviously pleased him. "Shall I go to him as an angry husband?"

"Oh, John! No!"

"All right, all right," Mannering riposted. "I'll go as a would-be counsellor and guide, and you go to Julie as a kind of mother figure. Darling," he went on, moving suddenly and taking her into his arms. "If it weren't for the murder here and the attack on you, this would really be fun!" He hugged her tightly as they stood body against body, he sought her lips and kissed her with fierce passion before drawing back, quite breathless. "I love you," he declared. "Since that time in Australia when I thought we had reached the end of the romance in our marriage, I have loved you more than ever." He kissed her again, drew back and went on : "That is a simple fact. Here is another. I don't own you, body and soul. I believe — you know I be-lieve — that there is a limit to self-denial and —" he broke off, drew his head back yet still held her close. "I needn't go on, need I?"

"No," Lorna said huskily. "No."

He kissed her more gently, and let her go.

During this time, Chief Inspector Willison was putting the results of his investigation down on paper, and there were two aspects of it. First, the murder at Mannering's flat and the attack on Lorna Mannering. Second, the mystery of the Fiora Collection. This was in an official re-port, which was now ready to be typed out. The key question was why the thieves were obviously convinced that Mannering had the jewels. It could be that, like the police, they had been tipped off by an anonymous telephone call : "If you want to find the Fioras, try Mannering at Quinns." Now that he was convinced that the jewels were not at Mannering's flat the possibility that they were at Quinns

had to be considered. The last paragraph of the report
read :

> There is no evidence on which to base a request for a
> search warrant effective at Quinns. Nevertheless, a search
> would be invaluable. I would be prepared to ask Man-
> nering for permission to search. If it were withheld then
> I might use the cuttings books as *prima facie* evidence that
> he might have in his possession jewels and *objets* stolen
> years ago. This would be thin but might reasonably be
> considered justification for obtaining a search warrant.

He would submit this to the Chief Detective Superintendent in charge of the investigation, and perhaps have it
passed on to the Commander, the Chief Executive of the
Criminal Investigation Department, who was responsible to
the Assistant Commissioner for Crime.

The second set of notes, not yet made as an official
report, were about Mannering's press cuttings books and
his interest in crimes most of which had been investigated
by Bristow, who had served the Yard for thirty years before
joining Mannering at Quinns.

Sitting at his contemporary-shaped desk in the square,
Was that so remarkable?

Reading through sensational newspaper reports of the
exploits of the Baron created a vivid mind picture of the
situation. Reading Bristow's reports of his investigations in
the 'unsolved' section of *Records*, showed that Bristow had
often suspected Mannering but had never obtained proof.
Yet after Mannering had bought Quinns, he had become
a consultant at the Yard! But despite frequent consul-
tation his own activities had often been investigated, by
Bristow helped sometimes by first Detective Sergeant, next
Detective Chief Inspector, now Chief Superintendent
Gordon, who had recently been put in charge of one of the
London divisions.

Before Willison committed himself to an opinion, he decided, he must consult Gordon.

bare office one wall of which was window, Willison picked
up the telephone, and said :

"Get me Mr. Gordon, of North West Division."

"I'll call you back," the operator said mechanically.

Willison rang off, and opened a folder with notes and reports on Tom Forrester and Julie Clarendon. Forrester
had inherited some two thousand pounds from his father
five years ago. He had been an art student for years, and
for some time had tried to earn a living by his painting.

"Queer stuff," Willison said to himself. "Damned queer."

Julie Clarendon's story was — although Willison did not
realise it — basically identical with what Bristow had told
Mannering.

Both of the young people appeared to be in the clear,
but there were the two factors which Willison thought were
of key importance : the indications that Mannering and
Julie were old acquaintances, and the fact that Lorna
Mannering had spent well over an hour with Forrester
that morning.

Willison's telephone bell rang; he expected Gordon, but
instead it was Detective Sergeant Joslin, of Fulham, the
man in immediate charge of the reconnaissance of the flat
in Riston Street.

"Yes, Joslin?" Willison was as aloof-sounding as ever.

"I've the final report on Mrs. Mannering's visit to
Forrester," Joslin announced.

"Let me have it," ordered Willison.

"They were together in the front room for at least half-
an-hour before going to the rest of the house," Joslin stated.

"On whose evidence?"

"The landlord's — the old man downstairs."

"And is he quite sure?"

"In his opinion they went to bed together," declared
Joslin. "He can't be sure, though. He says they talked for
a while and then fell silent. The next thing was floorboards
and bedsprings creaking, and a few minutes later they
were both on the landing."

"Do you think the old man is reliable?" asked Willison.

"He's got sex on the brain," answered Joslin. "I would say he's quite truthful but he might not interpret what he hears properly. He says this is what happens very often just after Julie Clarendon comes home from her office across the road. And there have been other women visitors who have followed this kind of routine."

"What conclusions have you reached?" Willison asked coldly.

"No conclusion, sir, but I'm sure of one thing."

"What's that?"

"If the old chap's got it right, then Mrs. Mannering has probably known Forrester for some time. But she's never been there before — at least the old man has never seen her and he doesn't miss much."

"What makes you think Mrs. Mannering's known Forrester for some time?"

"She isn't the kind who would jump into bed with a stranger!"

"I imagine you're right," Willison conceded, almost regretfully. "Put it all in your report."

"Very good, sir."

"Have you anything else on the Clarendon girl?"

"No, sir. No evidence at all that she's ever seen Mannering in Riston Street."

"Right," Willison said, and rang off.

There was no evidence at all that Julie Clarendon had seen Mannering anywhere — not even that she had visited Quinns before the previous morning. According to everything the police could find out, the statement that the couple had gone to enlist Mannering's help with Forrester's paintings was quite true.

After he had noted Joslin's reports, Willison's telephone bell rang again. This was almost sure to be Gordon.

"Mr. Gordon, please," he said.

"Mr. Gordon's on holiday in Switzerland," a man answered apologetically. "Chief Inspector Bell is deputising for him. Can he help, sir?"

"No, this is personal," said Willison, hiding his disappointment. "When will Mr. Gordon be back, do you know?"

"On Monday week," the other answered. "Sorry we can't help, sir."

"Can't be helped. Goodbye," Willison said mechanically, and rang off.

He sat back for a few minutes, staring out of the window. He couldn't wait to find out whether Gordon had ever had any grounds for suspicion; unless this case went sour on him, he would get results within a week. So he would have to use his own judgment. These old Baron robberies had for so long been on the 'unsolved' list that few men at the Yard would ever think of disinterring them but — could they be used to make the Mannerings talk? If not, to get that search-warrant for Quinns? Was it even conceivable that after the years in which the investigation had been dead and buried, that new evidence would enable him to do what Bristow and Gordon had failed, utterly.

If he could —

Willison's heart began to race.

He had jotted down a list of the jewels whose loss had been attributed to the Baron. There were fifty-one robberies with an average loss of £10,000 : over half a million in the values of twenty-odd years ago. The present-day value would be nearer two, probably three millions !

Proving who had stolen them, perhaps even getting some back, would be one of the greatest triumphs of Scotland Yard. If he succeeded he would become one of the key figures at the Yard, and his future here would be absolutely assured.

What other explanation could there be of Mannering's interest in these old robberies?

"I'm going all out to get him," Willison murmured aloud; and added slowly : "I am *going* to get him."

The direct way was to prove that Mannering had handled the Fioras recently.

Mannering was alone that evening, back in the study at

the flat. Lorna had to talk to a painters study group at one of the big London Colleges of Art; she should be home about ten. He was glad to have a chance to think. The more obvious danger from Willison had receded in his mind. No one was going to believe anything which might be raked up about the early robberies, and as there had been no evidence at the time of their occurrence there wasn't even the remotest likelihood that evidence could be found now.

So he pushed that possibility to the back of his mind.

The key mystery was the Fioras.

He stretched out for the telephone and flicked over the pages of the telephone directory. Sir Gordon Sangster, said to be so ill, had a small town house in Mayfair, and Mannering checked the number and dialled it, letting what he knew of Sangster pass through his mind. The man was a wealthy industrialist who had given large sums to different art foundations, to which generosity he owed his knighthood. He had always been a collector of jewels, and had been an occasional customer at Quinns for many years. Mannering knew he was a careful buyer, extravagant only where emeralds and rubies were concerned; but if he bought stolen jewels, he might well have one of the finest collections in the world : and a prize piece would obviously be the Fiora Collection. On today's market it must be worth a quarter of a million pounds. Could he have had it hidden away, all these years?

A woman answered and she sounded young.

"Sir Gordon Sangster's house."

"Is Sir Gordon there, please?"

"I'm afraid he's much to ill to speak to anyone," the woman replied.

"Oh, I *am* sorry," Mannering said. "I do hope he will soon be better."

"Thank you," the other answered quite formally. "Can I help you at all? I am his daughter-in-law."

"You're very kind," Mannering said, and hesitated as if not sure what to add. Then he went on : "My name is

Mannering — John Mannering, and this is a business matter. Who is handling his business — or rather the particular business of his collecting of precious stones?"

There was a long pause, before the woman replied in a much sharper voice:

"No one, I'm afraid. Goodnight." And she rang off.

Mannering also rang off, very slowly.

There wasn't any doubt about the change in the speaker's tone, or that his name had caused it. Why should Sangster's daughter-in-law be so sensitive; could she know that some of the jewels stolen from her father-in-law had not been lawfully his?

He telephoned Bristow, who answered so quickly that he must be sitting close to the telephone. For no particular reason, he felt enormously glad that Bristow worked for him, and that they had been so frank with each other that morning. Somehow it set the seal on their association.

"Bill, have you any reason to doubt that the Fioras inquiry is being kept quiet because Sangster himself is so ill?"

"That — and the fact that it suits the police," Bristow answered.

"Do you know anything about his son and daughter-in-law?"

"Just a few incidentals," Bristow answered, "and that only about the son. I was once at the Sangster house after a burglary and Bruce, the son, was there. He was about seventeen, at the time and had just been expelled from his public school — quite a minor one, as I recall. He'd already been expelled from at least two major ones. Sex and smoking, I gathered. Why, John?"

"Would he be about Tom Forrester's age?" asked Mannering.

"Middle twenties by now," Bristow mused. "So yes, they'd be of an age."

"Minor public school," Mannering remarked. "I wonder if it could have been the same school for each of them?

Whether young Sangster and young Forrester know each other?"

"It would be well worth finding out," Bristow said. "And that shouldn't be difficult, in the morning." After a pause, he went on : "Have you heard from Willison again?"

"No. Why?"

"He telephoned me about an hour ago and asked if I would go and see him in the morning. I know I'm under an obligation to help the Yard where I can, but they could overdo it, and if you'd rather I didn't I'll turn him down."

"You go," Mannering decided promptly. "We need to find out what's in his mind."

"I must say I would like to," said Bristow, in a voice which carried an overtone of uneasiness.

Mannering pondered Willison's activities for a few minutes after Bristow had rung off, but did not feel particularly worried. He was beginning to worry about Lorna, however. She wasn't exactly late, but it was already past ten-thirty. She was usually home much earlier. There was a general mood of uncertainty and disquiet, and he was probably over-sensitive. If she wasn't here within twenty minutes or so, he would telephone the Chelsea Art College, where —

The telephone bell rang.

"That'll be her, to say she'll be late," he said aloud, and picked the receiver up again.

"Hallo, darling," he said, so sure that it was her. "What time will you be home?"

"Never again, sweetheart," a man replied, "unless you're prepared to do a deal with me about the Fioras. I want a hundred thousand pounds for them and your wife, by noon tomorrow. I'll call you again when you've had time to think about it. Think *very* hard."

The man rang off.

15

Stand and Deliver

MANNERING SAT WITH THE receiver in his hand for a long time.

The shock had gone through him like a knife thrust, and he was only just beginning to recover. There was so much that he must do, but it was useless to start until he was in control of himself; and he wasn't, yet : he was actually trembling.

At last, he put down the receiver.

He stared at the lambent beauty of the brandy in the decanter near the telephone, and then at the glass by its side. Slowly, he shook his head. As slowly he looked up the number of the Art College, and dialled. A woman answered at once.

"Oh, yes, she left at the usual time, Mr. Mannering," she said. "But taxis were very difficult tonight. I'm sure she won't be long."

"Thank you," Mannering said.

He rang off, stood up and began to walk about the flat. It was useless to blame himself, but he should have gone to meet her, or at least made sure she didn't come home alone. She seldom did, anyhow, but walked most of the way with friends who attended the lectures.

Suddenly, he cried out : "My God, if he hurts her!"

He sat down on the edge of the chair, and dialled Bristow. This time there was a considerable delay, but at last Bristow answered, and he still sounded wide awake. As Mannering told him what had happened, his breathing began to get harsh, but he did not interrupt until Mannering finished. Then Bristow asked:

"What do you want me to do?"

"Telephone the Yard, and ask them if they can get my line tapped quickly," Mannering said. "Tell Willison, if you can get hold of him, that I'm going to do exactly what this man tells me, except that I can't give him the Fioras as I don't have them. The priority is to get Lorna back, but we must learn all we can in the process. If the police hear the demand then Willison is less likely to assume that I'm up to monkey business."

"I'll try him right away," Bristow said. "Shall I call you back?"

"No. I'd rather this chap can get straight through to me," Mannering said.

"I understand," Bristow said gruffly. "Shall I come over?"

"No, not yet," Mannering replied. "Thanks. I'll let you know when I need you."

He rang off. The ting! of the telephone sounded very loud, but at last it faded, the signal for the beginning of the period of waiting. The man who had telephoned had intended to let him sweat, of course; and not being over-demanding of money was clever. A hundred thousand pounds was not expensive for the Fioras alone, but — *Lorna.*

He clenched his teeth, and after a few seconds began to think more calmly and clearly about every aspect of the case. Where was the link between all the people involved? Who *were* they? He picked up a pencil and wrote out a list very swiftly.

1. Tom Forrester.
2. Julie Clarendon.
3. Jacob Walker (murdered at this flat).
4. Walker's murderer — whom he had photographed. (The prints had not been ready when he called for them)
5. Sir Gordon Sangster — and the Fioras.

6. Sangster's son and daughter-in-law.
7. The man who had telephoned Mannering.
8. Clive Paget and his wife, what was her name? Oh, yes. Doris.

Was there in fact a connection between all of these, or had the Forrester/Julie visit been a coincidence?

"No," he declared aloud. "The man was in their attic, and tried to kill Forrester. It's too much for coincidence. And there's no certainty that Paget is involved; and none that he isn't, either." He kept imagining a ting! at the telephone, but it didn't ring. At least the police should have had time to arrange for the tapping. The waiting was becoming unbearable, he must do something : anything —

There was the ting!

He snatched up the telephone and heard only the burring sound; no one was on the line. He kept the earpiece close, feeling almost stupid — and heard the *ting*! again.

It was the front door.

He placed the telephone receiver back, heavily, and stood up. The front door bell rang more loudly. He crossed to the room door and the hall in long strides, but hesitated before touching the door handle; at last he opened but kept the door on its chain to make sure that it could not be thrown back into his face.

He asked steadily : "Who is it?"

"Oh, Mr. Mannering," Julie Clarendon gasped. "Oh, John! Thank God you're in!"

Very carefully, Mannering looked out into the dimly-lit landing. He could see no one else; just the girl very close to the door. He unfastened the chain and opened the door wide enough for her to slip through, and as she came in he closed the door quickly and slid the chain into its slot.

Then he turned to look at Julie.

She was peering up at him intently, and her eyes seemed to glow. There was something both pathetic and appealing about her, but he was very, very wary, far from sure that she could be trusted. Before he spoke she moved, almost fell towards him, and he had to put out his arms to save her from falling. She huddled against him, her body so warm and soft, her silky hair just at a level with his chin.

She began to cry.

And she began to shiver.

He did exactly what he had done when this had happened before; changed his position, lifted her, and carried her off — not to the bedroom or the study, but into the big drawing room. Drawn up in front of the tall fireplace with its brass fire-irons and the beautifully wrought brass fire-screen was a long couch, and he placed her on this, and quickly drew away.

She looked so tiny, lying there.

And seductive?

She didn't move, but stared up. Her mini-skirt was rucked up high but not indecent by today's standards. Obviously she had been crying for a long time. Her eyes were red-rimmed, the curving lashes damp and stuck together, making her look forlorn.

"What is it?" Mannering asked quietly.

"I — I — I've nowhere to go," she sobbed.

"What's happened at Riston Street?" Mannering demanded.

"Tom's thrown me out."

"Nice man. Why?"

"He suddenly lost his temper, he just went berserk. He has before, he's threatened to throw me out before, but never —"

"Whoa back! Isn't it your flat?"

"That doesn't make any difference," she said miserably. "It's *his* home and workshop and studio."

"Don't you pay the rent with your typing fees?" demanded Mannering.

She nodded but didn't speak.

He had one ear alert for the ringing of the telephone, one listening to what Julie was saying. He was aware of the fact that if he were not so worried about Lorna he would be able to concentrate much more on Julie's story; on her 'plight'. There was no way of being sure that she was telling the truth, but what she said seemed in character for Tom Forrester. In one mood the great lover, in the next, the heartless brute.

When would the kidnapper call back?

"Do you mean he literally threw you out," he asked.

"Yes, the beast! I — I told him he was behaving like a pig to you and Mrs. Mannering, that he ought to tell you the truth, and — and he picked me up and carried me downstairs. Then he threw some clothes and things out of the window. I — I'd nowhere to go, and —" she faltered, then struggled up for the first time; the new sitting position made her even more provocatively attractive. "Where is Mrs. Mannering?" she sounded alarmed.

"She's out at a meeting," Mannering managed to say calmly.

"She — she will be back, won't she?"

Mannering made himself say: "Yes. Very soon."

"So I *can* stay, can't I?"

"What about your friends the Pagets?"

"*They* won't help," she stated scornfully. "They always do whatever Tom wants. They're his friends more than mine."

This didn't square with what Paget himself had said but there was no more reason to believe Paget than to believe Julie; there might be less. Mannering watched the girl closely as she sat still further upright, looking so very young.

He thought: Why doesn't the telephone ring?

He said: "Has he ever thrown you out before?"

"Not — not literally. He's talked about it often enough, though."

"Why didn't you have *him* thrown out?"

"Oh, please," she protested. "I can't. I simply can't. He's a — he *is* a genius. And I love him. I feel responsible for him. When people actually have real genius you can't apply the usual standards of behaviour to them." She was speaking now with great dignity and in a level voice. "If he were anyone else I wouldn't just live with him, I'd insist on marriage or nothing. Oh, I don't care on moral grounds but I don't believe men should get away with as much as they do. It — it's different where a genius is concerned."

Was she over-emphasising her belief that Forrester *was* a genius? Was she trying to fool him, Mannering, for some obscure reason? Or did she actually believe what she said?

He thought: Why doesn't the telephone ring?

He said: "What did you really quarrel about tonight, Julie?"

"The way he was behaving towards you, I tell you. The fact that he lied to you *and* Mrs. Mannering. I know he lied to her, he told me so."

"What about?"

"The — hanging attempt."

"*Was* it suicide?" demanded Mannering.

"No. Someone tried to make him talk, and — well, I got back and the man ran away. Or I thought he did. He must have stayed in the attic."

"Do you know what Tom was to talk about?" asked Mannering gruffly.

She said slowly, uncertainly: "Yes."

"Then why?" Mannering demanded.

"He's involved with some criminal, I don't know who. It's got something to do with jewels."

Mannering's heart began to thump and for the first time he forgot the telephone, all his attention concentrated on this girl. It was possible that she was telling the truth, not because of his questions but spurred on by her own anger and resentment.

"Who is the man he's mixed up with?"

"A — a thief."

"What thief?"

She said in a gasping voice: "A — a man Tom knows stole some jewels, a famous collection called — I *think* it was called the Fiona Collection." That name was very,

very close to 'Fiora' and some of the parts of his puzzle
began to fall into place, even the possibility that the attack
on him, Mannering, had been intended to frighten, not to
kill. "He asked Tom to look after them and Tom promised
to, and — and then he hid them away. After I'd got him
down he *was* conscious, and he told me what had happened. I — I drugged him so that he wouldn't be able to
talk to anyone else."

"Such as the police," Mannering said drily.

"It — it could be," Julie agreed. "He made me promise
to let everyone think it was attempted suicide so that no
one would suspect he had been attacked, and start asking
questions. He — he didn't want you or the police to think
that anyone had any reason to want to kill him."

"Oherwise, we would want to know why."

"That — that's right," Julie said, woefully. "That's exactly how Tom thought. I was against him coming to you
about the paintings, but I think he really wanted help over
this — this matter of the jewels. It was after you came to
the flat that I wanted him to tell you he truth. I said you
would almost certainly help him and in any case not give
him away. I started on it again tonight, that's when he lost
his temper and when —" Julie went on in a dreary voice
— "he threw me out. I didn't know where to go to, so I
came here. I *can* stay the night, can't I? Your wife won't
mind, will she?"

In a strangled voice, Mannering said: "No, she won't
mind." Then he thought: When is the telephone going to
ring?

On that instant, it rang.

He turned round very deliberately and went towards it,
while Julie sat without moving and watched him with
desperate intensity. He picked up the telephone, noticing
without thinking that the time by the mantlepiece clock
was twenty minutes to twelve.

He said: "Mannering."

"John," Lorna said in a steady but obviously strained
voice, "I'm quite sure that if you don't do what this man

wants, he will kill me. He says —" she seemed to swallow her words, but they became distinguishable again. "He says that he killed the man Walker, and that he's committed murder before. I'm in a room with him now, an ordinary kind of bedroom. I haven't — I haven't been molested, darling, but —"

The man's voice came clearly above hers drowning it, and there was menace in the tone: menace Mannering could not possibly fail to understand.

"That doesn't mean you won't be, sweetheart. If your loving husband doesn't think you're worth the money, I have to get something out of it, don't I?" Mockery sounded in his voice as he went on, obviously standing closer to the telephone: "She'll be all right, Mannering, if you do what I tell you. And you won't need a pencil, it's simple to remember. Take one hundred thousand pounds in cash to Tom Forrester's studio in Fulham. Hand it over to him. He'll be the messenger. I'll let him bring your wife back unmolested as she said. She will have the Fiora Collection with her. Believe it or not," he went on with the mocking note much more noticeable in his voice. "Twelve noon, on the dot, tomorrow. Don't be late, and don't try any tricks, such as going to the police. If I so much as smell a policeman, I will cut your wife's throat even if I have to cut my own as well." There was what seemed a very long pause before he said: "Your wife is very kissable, Mannering. Listen."

There was a moment's pause; and then the unmistakable sound of a kiss.

A moment later the speaker said, "Good night", and the line went dead.

16

Rendezvous

MANNERING STOOD BY THE telephone, without moving. He was oblivious of Julie, of where he was, of everything but the man's voice ringing in his ears, and of a picture of Lorna, graven on his mind. He could 'hear' the words: "I will cut your wife's throat, even if I have to cut my own as well." Except for the menace in it, it had been a pleasant voice. English. Public school.

Mannering became vaguely aware of sounds; rustling, creaking; and then he became aware of Julie standing in front of him, and staring up. And he heard her.

"John, what is it?" She caught her breath: "Oh, dear God, what is it?" She drew away from him as if his expression frightened her, and repeated beseechingly: "What *is* it?"

He drew in his breath and managed to keep his voice steady.

"My wife has been—kidnapped."

"Oh, no," she breathed. "No!"

He looked down on her as if she didn't really exist. Her prettiness, her elfin charm, her beautiful eyes. None of these counted for anything at all. He moved forward and she backed away. He clamped his hands on her shoulders and she began to struggle. She stared into his face and her fear grew into raw terror. She muttered something but it made no sense, unless it was 'please, please.' He shook her and her head bobbed to and fro. In a voice so hoarse he himself hardly recognised it, he rasped:

"What do you know about the kidnapping?"

She was gasping for breath.

"Nothing. Nothing. *Nothing*!"

He shook her again.

"Don't lie to me."

"I'm not lying," she said hoarsely. "I don't know anything about it. I wish —" she caught her breath and glared at him. "I wish to goodness I'd stopped him from coming to see you! If only he hadn't! Now — now look what's happened. He —" she began to clench her hands, to screw up her face. "He's thrown me out. He's actually thrown me out!" Now tears were falling and her body began to sway, she beat her breast with clenched fists. "I wish I'd never seen you. I wish I'd never heard of you! I wish —" she stopped suddenly and held her breath; then she flung herself at him, huddled against him and sobbed: "Oh, help me, please help me. I love him so!"

Mannering stood there, helplessly, holding her, not sure what to do — and the front door bell rang again.

She gave no sign that she had heard it but did not resist when he eased her away. He left her standing by the back of a winged armchair, but before he reached the front door the bell rang again. He hesitated, not sure whether to open it cautiously as he had before, or whether to pull it open sharply, catching whoever was outside by surprise.

From the landing, a man called: "John. Are you there? *John*!"

It was Bristow.

"All right, Bill," Mannering called out in relief, and glanced round as he opened the door. Julie was still crying. Bristow opened his mouth to speak but Mannering put his finger to his lips; open-mouthed, Bristow stepped in, and Mannering closed the door.

"Julie," he whispered.

"Good Lord!"

"What's brought you?"

"What brought *her*?" Bristow demanded.

"She says Forrester threw her out."

"I wouldn't trust either of them as far as I could see them," Bristow stated roundly. "I drove as far as the end of New King's Road and then called the Yard," he went on briskly. "They got your line tapped and heard that telephone conversation." When Mannering made no comment: "I'm desperately sorry, John. But you know that. I'm pretty sure Willison is, too. I had to come and tell you."

"What's Willison doing at the Yard at this hour?"

"He's a dedicated copper, remember. He'll come here if you think it will help."

"No," said Mannering sharply. "The place is probably watched."

"I was very careful," Bristow said. "And I saw no one."

"It could still be watched," Mannering replied. "I'd rather not chance it. Did Willison make any comment?"

"Only that he was extremely sorry and would do anything he could to help." Bristow gave a bleak smile. "And he also said he was now convinced that you hadn't got the Fioras, as this chap is trying to sell them to you." Bristow moved towards the drawing-room door. "Does the girl know what's happened to Lorna?"

"Yes," Mannering said. "I told her."

Julie was back on the couch, face downwards, head in her hands. She did not seem to be crying. Both men stood and watched her, but soon Bristow took Mannering's arm and led him to the study. He stood with his back to the fireplace, arms behind him, and looked at Mannering almost paternally; and his near-white hair and the lines on his face made him look old enough to be Mannering's father, although there was only twelve years between them.

"What are you going to do, John?"

Mannering said: "Pay if I must." He held his breath. "Pay, of course, rather than take the slightest risk with Lorna's life."

"Willison —"

"Bill," Mannering said. "I am not going to be guided by the police. I'm going to assess the situation and make my own decision about what to do. Then I'm going to do it.

If it means asking for police help, I'll ask. Meanwhile unless the men who've taken Lorna tell the newspapers, I'd rather there was no publicity — at least until after midday tomorrow."

"No reason why the Press should know," Bristow agreed. "What about the Clarendon girl?"

"Can you take her back and put her up for the night?" asked Mannering. "I don't want her here and I'd rather she was watched."

"I'll need to telephone my wife," Bristow said.

"Of course. Help yourself."

Bristow picked up the telephone, and Mannering went into the kitchen. This was really the first time he had been on his own since the telephone call, and the full effect of the threat hadn't yet hit him. It did now. He leaned against the door, covering his face in his hands; and all he could see was Lorna. His legs, in fact his whole body, went weak; trembly. He heard Bristow talking, followed by the ting of the telephone, which had a sharp effect on him; physical pain stabbed through him. Bristow came nearer, and called :

"That's all fixed, John." When Mannering didn't answer, Bristow appeared in the kitchen doorway. "Are you all right?"

"Yes," Mannering answered with an effort. "Yes, Bill. Thanks." He straightened up, forcing a smile.

Bristow drew a little nearer, frowning; he stood a couple of feet away from Mannering, and said very quietly :

"Don't take any chances yourself, John."

"I—won't."

"You look absolutely all in," Bristow said. "Is it any use suggesting that you take a sleeping tablet?"

"No use at all," Mannering said. "Take Julie away, please. What I need for the next few hours is time to think."

"John," Bristow said. "Don't go out tonight."

Mannering didn't respond one way or the other.

"You're not up to it," Bristow went on. "If you go out on your own you'll be asking for trouble."

"I won't ask for trouble," Mannering assured him.

Bristow hesitated, then turned away. His voice sounded very firm as he spoke to Julie. In a few seconds Mannering heard them in the hall, Bristow saying: "You can't stay here, but you can come with me." Julie didn't argue; they went out and the door slammed.

Mannering leaned against the sink for what seemed a long time. Then he began to do things mechanically. Fill electric kettle, plug in, switch on; get out cups and saucers — ass, he only needed one. *Oh God!* Get out light cream and sugar. Make instant coffee. Drink.

He knew exactly what he was going to do; Bristow knew, too. There was no possible way of evading it. He could no more stay here all night, doing nothing, than he could fly. The sweet coffee already made him feel better. He finished it and went into the passage between the bathroom and the bedroom. Above his head, very reminiscent of the hatch at Riston Street, was the entrance to Lorna's studio, with a wooden loft ladder leading up to it. He switched on a light on the wall down here, then went upstairs. This was a large attic, beautifully kept, with the smell of paint and turps everywhere. Dozens of portraits in various stages of completion lined the walls, from sketch-likenesses to nearly finished works. He went to an alcove where Lorna kept some of her paints, including a small, theatrical make-up set. He sat in front of a mirror ringed with naked light bulbs, and began to make-up. Although the first movements were mechanical, he gradually became absorbed as he used greasepaint, black powder, even spirit gum at the corners of his eyes, to alter his appearance completely. Next he put soft wax into his nostrils to broaden them, suction pads into his cheeks, to make them fuller.

Gradually, he became a different man to look at.

At last he finished, peered at himself, and was satisfied. He went downstairs again, took a sheet out of the linen cupboard, stripped, and wound the sheet about his waist, so making himself look quite corpulent. Next he slipped into some old clothes, normally too big for him but now too tight. The jacket had odd-shaped, sloping shoulders.

Once fully dressed, he went into the kitchen and shook some pepper on to a fold of notepaper and placed this carefully in an envelope; it was an old trick which often came in useful. Then he took a wad of ten pound notes from a hiding place in the roof, and at last went to the landing.

Instead of going down the stairs or down in the lift, he went upstairs to the roof, and climbed out through the sky-light. The stars were so bright they seemed almost within hand's reach. The air was crisp but not really cold. He walked over the roof to the next house, through that sky-light, down the stairs of a building identical with the one in which he lived.

He reached the street.

He saw a man in a porch some way along, and had no doubt that his house was being watched, and that had he been seen to leave there he would have been followed. He turned towards the Embankment and passed the porch, unable to see the other's face because of the shadows cast by low-powered street lights.

He was tempted to go up to the man.

The police detective stationed there to watch Mannering saw a heavily built man who walked with his shoulders hunched, one looking higher than the other, come out of the building next to Mannering's. He took no notice of him at all. For a moment he had a feeling that the other had seen him, was about to turn towards him, then changed his mind. The watcher took little notice, for his quarry was John Mannering.

Mannering reached the Embankment just after twelve-thirty; a church clock struck its chimes, sonorously, and they echoed over the still and silent surface of the Thames. No traffic flowed on the river and little motor-traffic moved

along the Embankment. Two taxis passed Mannering with
their signs alight, but he ignored them and began to step
out briskly; it no longer mattered whether he altered his
gait. He needed the walk in the fresh night air, and it
cleared not only his lungs but his mind. He could think
more dispassionately about Lorna, without making his heart
thump with sickening fear for her.

After fifteen minutes he turned into a narrow street, then
into another which faced the blank wall of a warehouse,
and in which there were some lock-up garages. He opened
the second of these with a key on his chain. Inside, just a
dark shape, was a small car : a grey Morris 1000, one of the
most common cars in Britain. He had kept a car of one
kind or another here for years; this, although second-hand,
was new to him.

It had a specially tuned engine which started at a touch.
He let it tick over for a few seconds while he checked the
tyres and the lights. Then he took a small tool kit packed
in a linen waist band; inside the waist band was a length
of nylon rope, quite strong enough to support his weight.
He wound this about his waist, took the wheel, and backed
out; he closed the garage door before driving off.

As he drove, he felt a different man.

He *was* now the Baron; he was nothing remotely like
John Mannering either to look at or in his mood.

And he was only a mile from Riston Street, and already
in Fulham.

He knew exactly what he was going to do.

Ten minutes after he had left the garage he parked
round the corner from Riston Street. No police were in
sight; they may have decided there was no need to keep
watch. There was a light at Number 20 and one upstairs at
Number 17, but none downstairs. He went to the porch,
taking a skeleton key out of his pocket, and slipping it into
the keyhole; after only a few moments of manipulation the
lock turned.

Using a skeleton key had once been virtually second
nature to him, and as he slipped back into the 'skin' of the

Baron, all the expertise he had once acquired with such care came back.

He stepped inside and closed the door; there was a faint sound of radio music from upstairs. He walked along the passage to the door at the end of the stairs, the one where the old man so often appeared. Immediately the door opened he heard a sound of snoring. A dim light was burning in a corner of the room, and the old man lay on his back, gnarled face clear in the light, cheeks sunken because he had taken out his dentures. Mannering took the key from the lock and went out, closing the door softly, then listened intently. The snoring went on without a break. Mannering turned the key in the door, and turned to the stairs and began to mount them.

The radio music sounded louder, but not really loud.

He reached the head of the stairs.

Lights were on in all the rooms, visible because the doors were open. The sound of music came from above, and footsteps sounded; so Forrester—or someone—was in the attic. Mannering stood close to the wall, listening, wondering if the man was coming down. He, the Baron, must wait for him; to go up would be to risk being seen and so put himself at great disadvantage.

No one was coming down.

Mannering went into the front room, which was exactly as he had seen it earlier. He searched in all the possible places where the jewels might be hidden, but found nothing. There was a hair-cord carpet fitted from wall to wall, and it showed no sign of being disturbed lately, so there was little likelihood that anything was hidden under the boards. Two old coffers, covered with padded seats, were unlocked; only blankets and linen and a few ornaments were stored in them.

Mannering searched the kitchen-living room, with the same result.

He heard the man whom he presumed to be Forrester moving about above his head, then heard the music more loudly, as if he were drawing closer to it. In fact, it was coming towards him : the man was carrying it as he started down the ladder now leaning against the hatch. Mannering stood so that he could see first the red socks, then the jeans, next the waist, finally his head and shoulders. The music now sounded very loud. Forrester rested a transistor radio on the water-closet cistern, and stepped to the floor.

That was when Mannering spoke in a hard, low-pitched voice, acquired years and years ago, and used only when he was acting as the Baron.

17

Struggle

"Stay where you are," Mannering ordered. "Don't turn round and don't move at all."

Forrester had one foot on the ladder, one on the floor; and his face was away from Mannering, his body in such a position that he could not easily look round. He seemed to freeze to the spot.

"I want the Fiora jewels," Mannering said starkly.

Forrester seemed to take in a deep breath before he responded :

"Come again."

"I want the Fiora jewels."

"*I* haven't got them."

"I don't believe you," Mannering said.

"I can't make you believe me," Forrester said flatly. "I can't give you what I haven't got, either."

There was a change in the tone of his voice as well as in his position. He was swivelling round with the foot on the floor, obviously getting ready to turn, perhaps to spring at the man he couldn't see.

"You have them," Mannering accused.

"You're wrong. You want a man named Mannering."

"*Mannering*?" echoed Mannering, as if the name shocked him.

"That's right, the great John Mannering, antique dealer, dealer in precious stones, consultant to Scotland Yard, and prince of crooks," Forrester growled. Then he twisted round on the ball of his foot and leapt at Mannering.

It was an act of cool, if reckless, courage. Had Mannering held a gun and fired, the other would not have stood a chance. As it was he came like a bullet, but all Mannering did was to step to one side and stick his leg out. Forrester ran into his leg and went crashing down, banged his head against the door, cried out, and flopped full length. Mannering moved swiftly and knelt astride the other, as if about to give him respiration, as for a drowning man. Instead, Mannering took his right wrist and pushed his arm up behind him, gave him a minute in which to recover his breath, and demanded :

"What makes you think Mannering has them?"

"I was told so," Forrester muttered.

"Who told you?"

"That's my business."

Mannering pushed his arm up tautly, painfully, and said :

"Now it's mine, unless you want a broken arm."

"You — you wouldn't dare !"

"I wouldn't trust me," Mannering said menacingly. "Who told you that Mannering had the jewels?" He increased his pressure, knowing he could not exert much more without breaking Forrester's arm. There was sweat on his own forehead and on the back of his neck, and his breathing was as rapid as Forrester's, although he tried not to let the other man know it. "You've one more chance : who told you Mannering had the Fioras?"

Forrester gasped : "A man named Paget."

"Who is Paget?"

"He — he lives across the street."

"How did he find out that Mannering had the Fioras?"

"He knew the thief who sold them to Mannering."

"So your friend Paget from across the street knows the thief and thinks Mannering bought the jewels from him. Is that it?"

"Yes !" gasped Forrester, and for the first time he showed some weakness; or at least, the effect of the pressure. "Don't — don't break my arm."

"I won't break anything if you tell me the truth."

"I've told you the truth!"

"Why did this Paget tell you about the Fioras?" Mannering demanded.

"I'd told him I was going to see Mannering about—about my paintings. He warned me to be careful, he said that Mannering was a crook."

"Oh, I see," Mannering said, with forced lightness. "He warned you for your own sake, did he?"

"Yes! That's what he told me!"

"Very generous of him," Mannering said with a sneer. "And Paget lives just across the street here."

"*Yes!*" cried Forrester again. "At Number 20."

"I want to see him," Mannering said. "I want to know why he thinks Mannering has the Fioras." He stood back, letting go of Forrester's arm gradually. "Get up," he ordered. "We'll go across together." He watched as Forrester climbed first to one knee, then the other; and saw the man's body go tense. He was ready when Forrester, on one knee, twisted round and flew at him again. This time, Mannering bent his knee and, with sharp and ominous impact, Forrester's chin struck the knee-cap. Mannering actually saw the other's eyes roll and knew that he became unconscious on the instant. Forrester fell, face downwards. Mannering paused only for a second before checking the other's pulse; it was fast but not abnormal. He hoisted Forrester up on to the W.C. pedestal, cut off a piece of the nylon rope and fastened the man by the ankles to the base, by the wrists to the water-pipe behind him.

This done, he turned away.

A moment later he listened at the door of the old man's bedroom, and heard the snoring as loud as ever.

He went out of the house, closed the door softly behind him, and stood in the porch. A car turned into the street from the Wandsworth Bridge Road and passed, headlights very bright; it turned a corner on Mannering's left. No one else moved. He went across the road and checked this door, it was a Yale lock, and trickier than that at Number 17.

This time he took a piece of high tensile steel out of the tool kit at his waist and inserted one end into the narrow gap between the metal lock and the side of the door. He pushed this through, slowly, and when the pressure was strong enough, each end of the steel jutting out equally on either side, the lock clicked back and the door sagged open an inch.

Mannering pushed it wider, and listened.

There was no sound.

He stepped in and closed the door, which would not lock, now; so he placed a chair against it, so that no one passing in the street could notice that it was ajar. He used a torch for the first time, since there were no lights on here.

All the downstairs rooms were empty. In the kitchen was the sour smell of unwashed baby linen. He already knew that the lay-out here was the same as that across the road; what he didn't know was how the Paget family slept. A very faint light showed about the frame of one door facing the stairs, and he saw that this was ajar. He pushed very slowly, holding his breath. It did not creak. Then he saw a nightlight at a bedside table, Doris Paget asleep in a single bed, the child in a cot, huddled in one corner.

Mannering found the key in the lock. He went out and locked the door, turned — and saw Paget in the doorway of the front room door.

Paget had what looked like a pistol in his hand.

The only sound was their breathing, and Paget's was coming so quick and shallow, clear indication that he was badly frightened; a frightened man might well shoot first and ask questions afterwards. Mannering kept his hands in front of him, obviously empty. Paget fought down his agitation and demanded :

"Who the hell are you?"

"I'm looking for the Fiora jewels," Mannering said, in the voice which no one who knew him would recognise.

"The hell you are !"

"That's right," Mannering said.

"What makes you think *I've* got them?"

"I know you know who has them."

"That's a lie!"

"Forrester told me that you told him."

"Like hell he did!"

"He certainly did. He said you said that Mannering of Quinns had them."

"That's right," Paget confirmed, changing his attitude immediately. "Mannering has."

"What makes you so sure?"

"I'm sure."

"I think you're a liar," Mannering said, roughly.

"My God. I'll shoot you if —"

"Because the police searched his flat and Bristow has access to his strong room, but nothing's happened to Mannering. If those jewels had been at the flat, they'd have arrested him. And Bristow might have resigned from the police and be working for Mannering but he wouldn't allow Mannering to keep stolen jewels at Quinns."

"Q.E.D.," sneered Paget. "Come in here and let me have a look at you." He backed further into the front room and switched on a light, which shone very brightly on to Mannering's face and on to the gun. *"Come on!"* He jerked the gun and Mannering did what he was told. He felt much steadier now, and quite sure that this man knew something. *"Get a move on!"* Paget ordered, and as Mannering crossed the threshold of the big room, he demanded: "What's your interest in the Fioras?"

Mannering said: "I've got a buyer."

"What do you mean, a buyer?"

"I mean another collector with more money than he knows what to do with, and a secret collection in an underground strong room in New York," Mannering said testily. "He'd pay a quarter of a million."

"Pounds or dollars?" Paget almost spat out the question.

"Pounds. Where are they, Paget?"

"I tell you . . ." Paget began.

"They're not at Mannering's, someone spread that story

around that they were so as to fool the police," said Mannering almost off-handedly. "Was that you?"

"You've got a nerve!"

"That's right," Mannering said. "And I've been living on strong nerves for a long time. I want those Fioras, and I'd split fifty-fifty with you or anyone else who's got them. Fifty-fifty," he repeated. "That's a lot of money."

"How do I know you're not lying?"

Mannering said slowly: "You don't, Paget. You just don't. But you've got a head on your shoulders, you know that two and two make four. I wouldn't come here and stick my neck out if I hadn't a good reason, and my reason's half of a quarter of a million pounds. I've been dealing in the hot jewels business all my life but I've never had a chance like this before. With that money I could retire." He waited and watched the different expressions chasing one another across Paget's face, ranging from doubt to hope and from hope to greed. The gun sagged, but this wasn't the time to take action; if Mannering made a false move now he could easily be shot and killed.

There must be no false move.

Whatever he did, all the time he must think of Lorna.

He said: "How about it?"

"I think you're lying," Paget said, and after a pause, he added: "What's the name of this buyer in New York?" The hope and the avarice were the emotions which showed on his face now.

"Topeski," Mannering answered promptly. "Cornelius Topeski. And if you don't believe he's interested, look at this letter —"

He put his hand to his inside breast pocket and took out the envelope.

As he did so Paget raised the gun and said: "Watch it!" Mannering opened the envelope and then tossed it negligently to Paget, who grabbed with his free hand. But before he touched it the pepper billowed out in a stinging cloud, and as he cried out in pain, Mannering leapt forward and knocked the gun out of his hand. It clattered to the

floor as Paget began to sneeze uncontrollably. Mannering
moved swiftly outside the room, and closed the door, listening. The sneezing was muted with the door closed and no
sound came from the other room.

Mannering went back, and closed the door softly behind
him, now in complete control.

He stifled a sneeze as pepper tickled his nostrils, but most
of it had settled on the floor and furniture. Paget stood
against the wall, his eyes streaming, sneezing violently
without stopping, pressing one hand against his stomach to
ease the strain on his muscles. Gradually, the paroxysm
subsided. He wiped his nose and dabbed his eyes, looking at
Mannering as if he were suffering from a dreadful cold.

At last, Mannering said: "Where are the Fioras, Paget?"

Incoherently Paget said something like: "I dunno."

Mannering raised the gun which he now held.

"There isn't any time to lie," he said, coldly. "You were
very interested in getting a price for them five minutes ago.
Who has them?"

"I swear, I dunno! I only know —" Paget began to talk
freely, as if the turning of the tables and the sight of the
gun had terrified him. His voice was thick and the words
ran into one another, but the gist of it was clear. He himself was in insurance. Often, he had to deal with claims for
stolen jewels, and this had brought him into contact with
fences and thieves. Two days ago a man had telephoned
and told him that he had the Fiora Collection and wanted
a good price for it; he had also said that he was going to
spread it about that Mannering was holding them.

"Why Mannering?" Mannering demanded.

"Doan ask me, I dunno," muttered Paget. "Just to put
the police off the scent, I dare say. Anyway, this man told
me to stand by, if I helped I would get a cut of the price
received. I just had to do what he told me, see. And he
told me to watch Forrester when I told him Forrester was
going to see Mannering."

"How did you know that?" demanded Mannering.

"Julie Clarendon told me," muttered Paget. "She said

she tried to stop him, but he had a bee in his bonnet about Mannering helping him with his painting. *Something* happened because Mannering went to the house across the street to see Forrester's paintings, or so he said. He came over here, too, to bring a message from Julie, who does chores for my wife. Julie couldn't come. I thought Mannering was interested only in Forrester's paintings, but it looks as if he was interested in something else."

Mannering asked, forcing himself to be patient: "Who is this friend of yours?"

"I don't know!" gasped Paget. "I swear I don't know! I —" he broke off, dabbing at his eyes again and began to snivel. "I sell insurance and settle claims, and he knows I okay'd an insurance claim once when I knew the real stuff was safe and paste imitations had been stolen. He — he put me on to it, and afterwards I had to do what he told me to, for fear he'd tell my company. I just had to do what he said."

"I want to know his name," Mannering insisted.

"I don't know his name, I tell you! There's only one thing I do know. He told me to tell Forrester to get Julie out of the house, that he wanted to do a deal with Mannering at Forrester's place tomorrow. He said Mannering would buy the Fioras for a hundred thousand quid, and I would get a thousand if I did what I was told. So I told Forrester and he kicked Julie out. She's not there any more."

"And all this just to allow Mannering to go and buy the Fioras from across the street?" Mannering said sceptically.

"Yes, I tell you, yes! This chap said Mannering had been there about the pictures, so Number 17 was a safe meeting place. And he told Forrester to stay in all day tomorrow until he got instructions."

"So Forrester also does what he's told, does he?" Mannering said grimly.

"This man's got some hold over him. Don't ask me what because I don't know" Paget was speaking more clearly although still hoarse from the pepper. "All I know is that

Mannering's going to be there to do a deal, a hundred thousand for the Fioras — and *you* know a man who'll pay a quarter of a million. Or are you lying?" Paget demanded, defiance breaking through his fear. "Are you lying?"

He glanced down at the envelope which had held the pepper, and then fearfully into the eyes of the man he did not know was Mannering.

18

The Plot

"Don't worry about that," Mannering replied in his most matter-of-fact voice. "I'm not lying." He moved to a hard-back chair and sat down; until that moment he had not realised how much he needed rest. He held the gun on his lap, the finger still in the trigger-guard. "*Do* you know what time Mannering is coming?"

"Twelve o'clock," Paget muttered.

"And Forrester will have the Fioras for him."

"I didn't say that." Paget was becoming more self-confident as the effect of the pepper wore off and as the danger from his own gun seemed to fade. "I said the exchange had to be done there, that's all. I don't know what part Forrester will have to play. Not much, I shouldn't think."

"Why not?"

"All that man can think about is daubing all over the place with sexy pictures," Paget said derisively. "I could have put him in the way of earning plenty of cash but he wouldn't go along with the idea."

"What was the idea?" demanded Mannering.

Paget answered without a pause to think.

"Doing copies of valuable paintings. That's a paying game, if you don't know it already. Big money paintings are copied at galleries and in private collections, and when there's a good chance, someone does a switch. There's always someone to buy at a good price on the underground market — like your client, Topeski, isn't it?" Mannering nodded. "I got on to this years ago, that's why I got to know Forrester. Let me tell you something," Paget went on, earnestly : "I moved in here when I knew Forrester was going to be at Number 17 all the time. That's why Julie's got a room here, for free. She baby sits sometimes but mostly I wanted to get a hold on Forrester, only it didn't work. I even offered him a lump sum down, whether his paintings made a profit or not — I knew they would sooner or later, mind you, I'm not Father Christmas."

For some incredible reason, Paget actually seemed pleased with himself.

"And what did Forrester say?" Mannering demanded.

"Some crap about art for art's sake. There's a lousy swine for you! He won't do a few pictures and make himself a good living because it's prostituting his art, but he'll live on that poor kid Julie. If she didn't earn enough for them both from her typing, they'd starve. And she waits on him hand and foot, buys the food and pays the rent, and what reward does *she* get? He throws her out. I tell you," Paget went on, with still greater indignation, "that's not a man, that's a womanising son of a bitch!"

Mannering, fascinated, asked quietly : "Can he do these copies?"

"Standing on his head."

"How do you know?"

"I've seen some," Paget answered. "Beauties they were — Vermeers and even a Rembrandt. He — my God!" breathed Paget, standing rigid with his hands stretched out in front of him. "That's the guy who's got him where he wants him. If Forrester did some paintings and they were switched with the genuine articles, anyone who knew about it would have him in a corner, wouldn't he? *Wouldn't he?*" Paget repeated in a shrill tone. "That's who the guy must be." He gulped, and moved forward, arms still outstretched, and Mannering raised the gun a fraction; but he did not think there was danger. Paget's still peppered-red eyes were actually blazing and his mouth was wide open; obviously he was speaking his thoughts aloud. "Listen, if we catch this guy doing a deal with Mannering over the Fioras, we'll have them both as tight as a wedge. Mannering *and* the guy with the Fioras. Why don't we work together, you and me? We could make a fortune!"

"I'm too old a dog to learn new tricks," Mannering replied, heavily. "I want these Fioras because I've got this ready market for them. Sure you don't know who's got them?"

"Not the foggiest," Paget insisted. "All I know is he's an old buddy of Tom Forrester, said he'd known Tom for years, they were at school together. That's another bloody racket, this old school tie business."

Mannering was very tense, but showed no sign of it. Old school tie; minor public school; Forrester and young Sangster. And another fact dawned on him, significant enough to threaten to choke him. Sir Gordon Sangster's was a collection of rubies and emeralds, *and* of Dutch paintings, mostly panels. He had several superb Vermeers. As these thoughts passed through his mind, he asked :

"What are you going to get out of tomorrow's deal?"

"Between this guy and Mannering?"

"Yes."

"A thousand quid. I told you."

"It's not worth the risk," Mannering declared.

"What is worth it, then?" demanded Paget, breathing more heavily. "Come on, tell me. What is?"

"Helping me to lift the Fioras when they're at Forrester's place," answered Mannering.

"How much is in it for me?"

"Five per cent of what I get — and a thousand as a starter the moment I've got my hands on them," Mannering offered. He put his hand to his pocket again, waving the gun carelessly. "Here's a hundred to show earnest." He took the wad of notes from his inside breast pocket, and tossed it on to the foot of the bed. "Take ten of those, if it's a deal," he ordered.

Paget counted the notes out with great care, then

shuffled the others together and pushed them nearer
Mannering.

"Oh, it's a deal all right," he said, almost crowing. "But
we've got to be careful."

"I'll be here at ten o'clock in the morning," Mannering
told him. "I'll have the details all worked out by then."

"Okay!" breathed Paget. "Okay. You going now?"

"Yes."

"Don't make any noise," pleaded Paget. "We don't want
to wake the kid."

Mannering stepped into an empty street where the lamp-
light shone on the roofs of the cars; there was hardly a
parking space left. No lights showed except at Forrester's
place. He forced that lock again, and stepped inside. The
old man's snoring was now so loud that Mannering did
not need to go close to the door to check it. He glanced
into the other two downstairs rooms, which had a few
sticks of furniture but were otherwise empty, then went
upstairs cautiously; but there was no need to worry;
Forrester sat where Mannering had left him, his head leaning against the wall as if he were trying to get some sleep.
He did not stir as Mannering climbed the stairs, which
were surprisingly solid in such a small house. Mannering's
mind was much clearer and he knew exactly what he
wanted to do. The anxiety for Lorna nagged like toothache
and a false move now could bring about her death.

He felt differently about Forrester, virtually convinced
that painting was his life, that he wanted above all to make
his living by his own creative work. He looked tired and
drawn. His mouth was slightly open, his chin, thrusting,
looked very long and pointed. Mannering went closer and
studied him intently from several angles, then tip-toed out
and into the lighted kitchen. Over by a plate rack were four
self-portraits, all in coloured crayons, and another in water-
colours. Mannering took these down and placed them at
the head of the stairs, then went back to the bathroom.
Forrester hadn't stirred.

"Forrester," Mannering said quietly, but to no effect.
"Forrester!" There was still no response. He touched the
man's shoulder, and for the first time Forrester moved,
stiffening; and his eyes flickered. "Wake up," Mannering
said sharply, and when the other sat up sharply, he rasped :
"How much did Bruce Sangster pay you for painting those
copies of Vermeer?"

The words seemed to hum about the room. *Vermeer—
meer — meer* echoed. Forrester's eyes opened wide, his
mouth dropped open, his expression was one of extreme
incredulity.

"*How much?*" demanded Mannering. "If you want to
get free of him, tell me." When Forrester made no answer,
probably because he was so shocked, Mannering growled.
"I could break your neck. Or your fingers, one by one.
How much did he pay you?"

Forrester drew in a deep breath, and then answered in a
strangled voice : "Two-fifty each." He stared at Mannering
as if at a freak, and managed to say : "Who — who the
devil *are* you?"

"Never mind. Why did you throw Julie out tonight?"

"How do you *know*?" breathed Forrester.

"Why did you do it?"

"I — I had to." There was a pause before Forrester went
on : "Sangster made me."

"What made you obey him so readily?" Mannering
sneered.

"He wants her out of the flat so that he can be here
tomorrow, and he doesn't want to be recognised. He — he
can—he can tell the police about me."

"For the Vermeer copies?"

"Yes."

"It's no crime to copy a picture, no crime to sell it—the
only crime comes if you try to pass if off as genuine. Didn't
you know that?"

"No!" gasped Forrester. "I swear I didn't."

"And that was all he had on you. There's nothing else?"

"I — I stole some paints and brushes, and he found out,"

said Forrester. "And —" he moistened his lips. "If I don't do what he says, he'll throw vitriol over Julie." Forrester was gulping time and time again; one gulp for every few words. "He — he'd cut off my right hand."

"Nice chap," Mannering said, in his own and not the Baron's voice, but Forrester did not seem to notice the slip. "So you're going to do what he tells you?"

"I haven't any choice," Forrester said bleakly. "I sent Julie away because I was sure she'd go to Mannering — do you know Mannering?" He flashed that question cunningly.

"Yes," Mannering answered.

"If I'd told her to go to him the obstinate little witch wouldn't have, but on her own that's where she'd go. And I'm sure Mannering will look after her if anybody can. And — there's some other job Bruce wants done tomorrow. He's going to meet Mannering here, he wants him to buy some stolen jewels."

"*Mannering* buy stolen jewels," Mannering rasped, incredulously. "Not on your life."

"Bruce Sangster says he will."

"Then Sangster's a fool," Mannering said. "Do you have a picture of him?"

"There — there are one or two sketches in the living-room," Forrester said, and tried to get up, as if he had forgotten he was tied. He dropped back again. "If you would cut me loose, I'd be able to show you. I wish to hell I knew who you were."

"I am a fence," Mannering said, with great deliberation. "And I've a safer market for the Fioras than ever Mannering would be. You want to be free, you say?"

"Of course I do."

"I'll untie you if you'll leave here without any fuss when I do."

"But I've got to be here —" Forrester began desperately.

"You were right, Julie did go to Mannering," Mannering said. "Then he sent her to his manager's home, an ex-Yard man's. She'll be safe there. So will you, if you've the guts to go and take your chance."

"But I must stay here!"

"What chance do you really think you'll have with Bruce Sangster?" demanded Mannering. "Do you believe he'll ever loosen his grip? Or don't you think he'll pretend to, and whenever he needs you, will come back and threaten to blackmail you again for your share in all this. Isn't that what he'll do?" Mannering thrust his face closer to Forrester's.

"I — I expect so."

"So if you're not here when he comes —"

"I must be! If I'm not he'll give me away, and — oh, God, you don't know him. If he says he'll do a thing, he'll do it. He's absolutely ruthless — a devil if ever there was one. He's robbed his own father for years, he keeps the old man virtually a prisoner in his sick-room. He — he's utterly heartless I tell you!" Forrester was sweating now, and spluttering. "I must be here."

"I must be here," Mannering said. "I'll deal with Bruce Sangster, not you. Now stop arguing and do what I tell you." He took a pen-knife from his pocket and cut through the nylon cord at the other's wrists and ankles. At first Forrester couldn't stand without swaying but gradually the circulation began to make him tingle, and he was able to move about. He led the way into the kitchen-cum-living room and pointed to four pencil sketches of a young man. They were tucked away behind a cupboard and Mannering hadn't seen them before.

"There's Bruce Sangster," Forrester stated.

He pointed at the man who had turned to look upwards after running away from Mannering's flat: from Jacob Walker's murder. And tomorrow there would be a photograph to prove he had been in Green Street.

"Forrester," Mannering said quietly, "you've one chance of freeing yourself from Sangster now and for always. This is it. Mannering's manager will put you up, too, if —"

"How do you know so much about the manager?" demanded Forrester.

"It's my job to know," Mannering said calmly. "I will drive you there, and you'll find Julie there already. Then all you have to do is wait."

Forrester muttered : "It's taking a hell of a chance."

"Tell me of any other chance you have," Mannering retorted.

Their eyes met for what seemed a long time, and then Forrester raised his arms and let them flop. He did not notice the drawings at the head of the stairs, and Mannering picked them up and slipped them under his jacket. Soon, they were in the Morris 1,000. At one end of Putney Bridge Mannering left the car to telephone Bristow, and Forrester made no attempt to escape; it was as if he realised that he had reached the crossroads, that he must take this chance of freeing himself from Bruce Sangster's stranglehold.

On the telephone, Bristow said : "Yes, John, we can put him up on a couch. All you want me to do is keep them both here until after mid-day tomorrow."

"That above all," Mannering said earnestly. "Until I give the all clear."

"All right," Bristow promised. "I should have known better than to try to prevent you from working on your own. Does Forrester know who you are?"

"No."

Bristow said : "You think Sangster is holding Lorna, and you're going to be at Riston Street, instead of Forrester, when Sangster comes. Is that it?"

"Yes," Mannering said.

"John, if you were to tell Willison —" Bristow began.

"Bill," interrupted Mannering, "if I tell Willison he's likely to raid Sangster's house, or at least watch it; and that will tell Bruce Sangster that the police are suspicious. I'm not prepared to take the risk. He's a cold-blooded killer who will probably rather kill himself than be caught and imprisoned." He had a vivid mental image of Forrester's face as he had talked of young Sangster; another, of the face of the man himself as he had run along Green Street. "If I thought there was a chance I'd go to Sangster's house myself, but I won't take the risk that he might kill Lorna."

Bristow said gruffly: "I know exactly what you mean."

Mannering rang off and went back to the car. Forrester was staring straight ahead, tight-lipped. He was still tight-lipped when Bristow opened his apartment door for him, while downstairs, Mannering drove away from this huge complex of flats halfway along Putney Hill.

Bristow took Forrester to the door of the spare-room, where Julie was sleeping; then he closed the door on her and showed Forrester to a long, comfortable-looking couch.

They were both sleeping, Julie and Forrester, when Bristow went to bed.

Mannering was aware of policemen watching him as he drove away from Bristow's, but no one followed. There was little traffic about, but all the street lamps were misted with a light drizzle. He hadn't yet decided where to go: to Green Street, back to Riston Street, or to the East End, where he had an old friend who was a make-up artist, as near a genius as could be.

Fear for Lorna was like a cancer in his mind.

The waiting was almost intolerable. But he had to wait for Bruce Sangster to make the first move. If things went wrong at noon tomorrow he could alert the police, but Sangster had to leave his house and go to Riston Street before the police took any action, otherwise they would almost certainly move too quickly.

Was she at Sangster's house?

Was she asleep, or wakeful and fearful?

Was she alone?

The urge to go to the West End, break into the house and find out the truth grew stronger all the time. But he fought it away. The one real hope was to impersonate Forrester, and he must not rely on himself to put on the Forrester disguise; it had to be perfect. He must go to the make-up artist who lived in Whitechapel.

As he drove along the Embankment, Mannering saw the illuminated dial of Big Ben; it was nearly a quarter to two.

In a little more than ten hours, he would come face to face with Bruce Sangster.

19

The Fiora Collection

"Mr Mannering," said old Pendleton, who had worked on disguises for Mannering for nearly twenty years, "I am delighted to see you." They were in a small room rather like a theatrical dressing-room, in his small terrace house near Whitechapel Church. He was small and old and wizened. "And I take the liberty of an old friend."

"Tell me," Mannering said.

"You are very tired."

"Yes," Mannering admitted. "But I still have a lot to do."

"In the morning, I can make you this man's double," declared Pendleton. "It will take only two hours. If you will now sleep until half-past eight, I will guarantee to wake you in good time."

"I doubt if I shall sleep," Mannering demurred.

"Then you should take a little white tablet which I will give you, with some warm milk and a lacing of brandy —" Pendleton broke off, appealingly.

"All right," Mannering conceded. "I'll be sensible."

If he slept, he told himself, he would forget for a while.

He slept; soundly.

In a small box-room at Sangster's house Lorna slept, fitfully; she was locked in, there was no window, but at least she was not bound to the bed. In another room Bruce Sangster slept with his wife, and on the same floor, his aged father was more in drug-induced coma than in sleep itself.

At Bristow's apartment, both Forrester and Julie slept well.

In Riston Street, so did the Pagets and, across the road, the old man with his snoring.

"A little more hair on the left sideburn, yes," said Pendleton. "And a snip or two on the back of the head. How well your hair has kept its strength, Mr. Mannering . . . Now, let me look at your ears. You need some wax, but that is no problem." Deftly, the old man worked on the outside and the lobe of an ear, glancing frequently at one of Forrester's self-portraits emphasised the ears and the temple. "He is a remarkably gifted young man, this artist. I think he uses fewer strokes with pencil or brush than any I know and yet he is not careless or pop. Oh, this modern pop art!" He stuck the extra wax on to Mannering's ear with an odourless liquid glue. "Excellent! . . . Such talent, so often wasted in protest . . . Now, the other ear." He fashioned another lobe, and added: "There is a slight scar which I shall have to simulate. How good will the light be, Mr. Mannering? . . . Not too bright? Good! And how long must the disguise last? . . . Only a few hours? That is easy. Now had you answered by saying a few *weeks* that would have been different . . . Now, a waisted sheepskin jacket, blue denim shirt, a pair of Levis, and you will pass for this young man even to those who know him well, but the impersonation would have to be short-lived . . . Good! Now, see for yourself," he urged.

Mannering stepped forward so that he was enclosed on three sides by a mirror. And even he was startled at the change which had come upon him.

He looked like Tom Forrester in the face and head and shoulders, but was too thick at the waist. As he smoothed his stomach, Pendleton said: "I can lend you a rubber stretch belt, which will help you there."

The belt made Mannering's stomach and hips not only flat but deceptively slender, yet was comfortable to wear.

Soon Mannering was driving across London.

At half-past eleven he left the car a few hundred yards away from Riston Street, in Wandsworth Bridge Road, walked past a little parade of old shops, turned into the street and went straight to Number 20. The door opened as he pushed the gate, and Paget stood there, in obvious agitation.

"What do you want?" he demanded.

"A word with you, Clive." Mannering spoke in Forrester's voice, accurately enough to get by.

"I can't. I've a visitor coming."

"I won't keep you five minutes," Mannering said, and pushed the other inside. "Where is Doris?"

"She's gone to her mother's for the day." The man was too much on edge to notice that this 'Forrester' was a larger man; and the danger-moment was past.

"That's good," Mannering said. "And now, Clive old boy, I want to know what you've been up to lately. You're working with Bruce Sangster, aren't you? Come on, tell me," he repeated roughly. He took Paget's right arm and twisted it behind him, thrust him forward and up the stairs. Paget kept kicking against the treads, he was so terrified. Mannering pushed him into the bathroom, tied him hand and foot as he had Forrester the previous night, and then slapped a piece of adhesive tape over his lips. "I'll be back for you," he said roughly, and stepped out, closing the door.

He went to the front room.

A few people were in the street, including two women on their doorsteps and three younger women pushing prams, one with hot pants which showed every curve imaginable. There was no sign of activity at Number 17 and he reached the door and took out Forrester's keys. Before he found the right one, the door opened and the old man backed away, as if in sudden alarm.

"Might as well kill a man as frighten him to death," he

complained. "And where have *you* been? Had two messages for you, I have. I thought you were never coming back." His rheumy old eyes were surely too weak to let him suspect that this was not Forrester.

"I've been out about some painting," Mannering answered briskly. "Who are the messages from?"

"A Mr. Bruce," the old man answered. "He said he'll be here at a quarter to twelve, and if that Mannering comes, he's to stay. What's on?" The frail voice then became gruff, the man thrust his face closer to Mannering's and asked: "What's up? You having some luck at last? Eh? Tell me, Tom boy, are you breaking through?"

"I'll break through before I'm finished," Mannering said sharply.

He broke off.

That was the moment when he realised that he didn't know the old man's name. At the back of his mind there was a name ending in Ed. Fred, Ed, Ted, something like that, but he couldn't be sure. So he had to phrase his comments so that he need not use any name.

"What's up?" the old man demanded. "What's up with you today, Tom, boy?"

"I'm sick of myself," Mannering said. "That's what's up."

"Why, what have you done, Tom?"

"I kicked Julie out. Isn't that enough?" Mannering was on edge to get away not only from the cross-examination but from the pale grey eyes. They had a shrewdness which troubled him, a directness which might well pierce the disguise. *Nonsense!* thought Mannering, and pushed his way past the old man; it was darker in here, but he need not worry too much, for his back was to the daylight; no one could possibly scrutinise him in such a light.

"You don't have to worry about Julie," the old man scoffed. "She'll come running back at a crook of your finger."

"I'm not so sure," Mannering said. He was now

between the other and the stairs. What *was* that name? Ed, Ted, Fred, — *Ed*, he was sure. "Are you going to be out for long?"

"Only going to get some baccy," the other said eagerly. "Like me to open the door when Mr. Bruce comes?"

Again, Mannering was caught in two minds, not being sure which was the usual thing to happen. The old man probably smelled a smile, which meant money, hence his friendliness. There was no point in making him hostile, and even if he didn't open the door he would peek from his own room to see who it was.

"Not until I call down to say it's all right," he said.

"Of course, Tom, of course! Don't worry at all. You just give a shout and I'll open the door."

Mannering went upstairs as the street door closed. Now he had the flat to himself, but could not be sure for how long — nor how much longer he must wait. Had he done anything wrong? Would he have been wiser to allow the police to watch here, or at least to watch Sangster's house? Nonsense! The risk to Lorna would have been too great. When he had her back he could take any risks; but not yet.

It was quarter past eleven; he probably had half an hour to kill.

Kill.

He moved about the living room, studying the portraits, even more impressed by their skill. It might be simply virtuosity, there might not be a real streak of genius, but most were good. Among the best were some of Julie, two of them little gems.

Never mind Julie! She was safe.

He heard someone come in, went to the stairs to make sure who it was, and saw the small grey head with its bald spot. Now it was simply a matter of waiting and there was only one place to wait : in the front room. He pulled a chair close to the side of one window from which he could see the Wandsworth Bridge Road end of the street; he took it for granted that Bruce Sangster would come from that end. Suddenly, a small motor-cycle turned into Riston Street, and slowed down. A man in a black jacket and a crash helmet painted white with a red emblem on it, began to peer about him, at the numbers.

He stopped, parked the machine, and walked towards Number 17, taking his helmet off as he moved. For the first time, Mannering was sure beyond doubt that this was Bruce Sangster, who looked younger than his years in this outfit.

Sangster disappeared from sight, beneath the window. After a moment, there was a loud bang on the iron knocker. Mannering heard a shuffle of feet downstairs, and the old man appeared at the door.

Fred : that was his name. *Fred*.

"Let him in," Mannering called.

"Right, right," the old man called up.

Mannering stood in the bathroom doorway. He heard the street door open, then the old man speak in his querulous voice.

"Yes. Who is it?"

"My name is Sangster," the caller replied, "and I've come to see Mr. Forrester."

"Old Tom boy? He's upstairs, unless I'm much mistaken. Tom! Tom, boy!" Fred raised his head as he peered upstairs, but Mannering hardly noticed him, he was so intent on Sangster. "Tom! It's a Mr. Sangster for you."

Mannering made himself call : "Ask him to come up." He opened the front room door wide, and then went to the head of the stairs. Sangster came up quickly, and the angle at which Mannering saw his face was exactly that from which he had seen it in Green Street.

It was gloomy on the landing, but Sangster's eyes seemed very bright.

"Hi," he said briefly. "Did you do what I told you?"

"Yes," Mannering answered.

"I didn't think you'd make any mistake." There was a sneer in the other's voice, a sneer on his heart-shaped face. The worst thing about him was that he was so evil yet had the face of an angel. There was a fringe of curly

golden hair and an angelic expression until one saw the
tautness and the thinness of his lips. "Mannering will show
up in twenty minutes."

"You seem very sure."

"I *am* sure," Sangster said, icily.

"I don't see how —" Mannering began.

"You never could see further than the end of the nose
on your face," Sangster sneered. "The jewels would be
enough in themselves, but I made doubly sure." He actually
laughed. "I kidnapped his wife! And he'll come along for
her sake. When he does, he'll get a hell of a shock."

Sangster laughed again, and Mannering felt icy stillness
in his veins for he did not know what this man meant,
knew only that he was most certainly in the presence of
evil. And it *was* evil. Everything he had heard about this
young man had pointed towards that, and here he was,
the personification of it.

Mannering made himself speak in a fair imitation of
Forrester's voice.

"What kind of shock, Bruce?"

"A hell of a shock," repeated Sangster, and for a moment
it seemed as if he were not going to explain. But at last
some sense of vanity, of boastfulness, perhaps of pride in
himself, rose to the surface, and he went on : "From now
on, he and I are partners. I've a tape recorder here." He
took a small transistor-type recorder from his coat and
placed it on a bedside table. "Our deal for the Fiora
Collection will be recorded. *My* voice won't be on it. Yours
will. Yours and Mannering's, doing a crooked deal. Once
I've got that on record you'll both do whatever I tell you.
You'll work for Mannering. When I tell you to paint a copy
of an old master, you'll paint it and he'll sell it as the
genuine article. And when I want to pull off a deal in
objets d'art or jewellery or antiques, he'll co-operate. If he
doesn't or if you don't —"

Sangster broke off; smiling. It was like a leer; satyrish.
But it was much more than that : he was not dealing with
an ordinary man but with a psychopath.

"You — you swine," Mannering made himself say.

"So I'm a swine. So you're a fool. You let me get a hold on you when we were at Letts together, and you'll never be free. That will teach you not to steal from lockers. You'll live your life the way I want you to from now on. From *today* on. So will Mannering. And he'll stand to lose more than his reputation, too. That wife of his is quite a woman. If Mannering makes trouble, his Lorna will pay. Only remember one thing, Tom." He gave his biggest smile yet. "Don't call me a liar. I don't like it."

Without the slightest warning, without any change in his smile, he struck Mannering savagely across the face. Mannering staggered back. Sangster, as if completely sure that he was in no danger, moved towards the window.

"He should be here soon," he remarked. "I'd better be ready to show him I mean business."

Mannering, teeth clenched, anger raging through him, saw Sangster slip his hand inside his jacket and then draw off his waist a leather belt or waist band, about six inches wide. He placed this on the bed and unrolled it, much as Mannering might have unrolled his tool kit. It stretched three feet up the bed, at least. He unfolded it, doubling its depth, and on that instant the morning light touched the jewels there.

Mannering caught his breath.

All his life he had worshipped precious stones; even today they exerted a near fatal fascination for him. He longed to touch, to stare at, to possess. And here was one of the most beautiful and varied collections of rubies and emeralds in the world. One ruby was the size of a pigeon's egg. Two rubies were nearly as large. They seemed to glow and to sparkle; to absorb light and yet to scintillate. They were set in rings, ear-rings, brooches, pendants, bracelets — there was a comb set in gold and fit for any queen. Mannering felt the magic, near magnetic attraction of them; they even affected his breathing.

"Look out of the window and see if he's coming,"

Sangster ordered. "He's late already. He'll have to learn that I don't like being kept waiting."

Mannering did not move towards the window, but instead stood between Sangster and the landing door. Sangster, surprised, took a step forward.

"Mannering isn't coming," Mannering stated. He had never felt less like himself, or more like another personality altogether, so absorbed was he in the part he was playing. "You aren't going to get your evidence, Bruce. Roll those jewels up again and give them to me."

As he spoke, as the stupefaction crept over Sangster's face, he took an automatic pistol out of his pocket, waved it towards the other, and went on sharply.

"Do what I tell you. I don't like being kept waiting, either."

Sangster stood absolutely still. His expression seemed to say : 'You must be mad !' Actually he said : "Mannering will be here at any moment, and —"

"No he won't," Mannering retorted. "I'm here in his place. And the police will be here before you've had time to get over the shock. They'll be at your father's, too — everywhere you might try to run to earth. You've been run to earth already, Bruce. Here. By *me*. You tried to push me around too much, and you had to be stopped. Mannering showed me how to stop you."

"Why, you —" began Sangster, and leapt forward, his mouth wide open and his eyes rounded and glaring.

Mannering fired at him.

The bullet actually went through the padded shoulder of the coat, but Mannering did not think it touched the flesh. The sharp report and the flash made Sangster back away, danger and fear of death overcoming his fury.

Mannering thought : It's nearly over, thank God. It's nearly over.

And that was the moment when the old man spoke from the open doorway. His voice was firmer and his manner more authoritative than it had ever been as he said :

"Drop your gun, Tom. Drop it on the bed and don't turn round."

Sangster said in a throbbing voice : "Nice work, Fred."

'*Fred*'. "Very nice work. Now the first job is to find out whether he's telling the truth about the police."

Mannering dropped the gun.

This was the first time since the affair had started that Mannering had felt really afraid for himself. And sick at his own blindness. Grey-haired old *Fred* was the wheel on which these crimes had turned.

20

Double

HE COULD NOT BE sure that the old man had a gun, but he could not take the risk of guessing wrong. He was acutely and vividly aware of Bruce Sangster's expression, and the naked evil in it. He did not doubt that Sangster would be viciously violent in order to find out what he wanted to know, but that in itself was unimportant. When he *was* convinced, he would get away as fast as he could.

And he would kill without compunction; once caught he would get a life sentence for Jacob Walker's murder, and one more killing would make no difference.

He moved close to Mannering, and without blinking his eyes, struck him across the cheek with his right hand, sending him reeling, then striking him with his other hand, just as viciously. Mannering's head rang, and he began to sway. He gritted his teeth and struggled to keep his balance. Sangster's face was going round and round, nothing about him seemed to stand still.

"Are the police really on their way?" he demanded, harshly.

Mannering said : "They're on the way."

Sangster raised his hand to strike again but old Fred moved past Mannering, making the blow impossible. He held a small automatic in his right hand, with a kind of nonchalance which suggested that he was not unaccustomed to it.

"It's no use knocking his block off," Fred reasoned. "You can't make him speak the truth if he can't speak at all, can he, Tom? Now, let's have the truth — every bit of it, Tom boy!"

In this room the light from the window was good. Both men, who knew Tom Forrester well, stood only a foot or two away, scrutinising him closely, searching his face for signs of the truth. They would not be fooled by the disguise for long, and once they realised that he wasn't Forrester but Mannering, they might well tear him to bits. There was one hope and only one, and he drew a deep breath and used that hope.

"I am not Tom Forrester," he said. "Tom is on his way with —"

They realised that truth on the same instant. Both of them flinched, physically, and for a split-second they were off their guard. Fred's gun actually pointed towards the floor.

Mannering sprang backwards.

Going forward would give them a chance to recover. Going backwards might save him. And Fred had left the door wide open. As he rocked on his heels Mannering caught at the door with his right hand. As he staggered on to the landing, it slammed. Simultaneously, two shots rang out, one sharp, one a roar; the two men had recovered at the same moment. The door closed tight but there was no time to lock it. Mannering darted into the bathroom and slammed that door; his fingers, icy cold, kept steady enough for him to shoot the bolt.

Two more shots followed. One bullet splintered a door panel, one made a bulge above the lock, but neither penetrated fully. Mannering put one foot on the decorated pedestal, both hands on the edge of the hatch, and hauled himself up, remembering the low rafters and keeping his head low. He heard the bathroom door groan and creak as he backed away, pulling at the hinged hatch cover. He caught a glimpse of Sangster darting into the bathroom as the hatch slammed down.

Then he stood on the hatch cover, to prevent it from being pushed open.

It began to heave beneath him as Sangster pushed, but Sangster had no chance while all Mannering's weight was on it. Again Mannering gripped a rafter, for support. Now that this part was virtually over, reaction had set in. He kept his mouth open and let his teeth chatter and his body shake.

Sangster was screaming at him but there was no sound of Fred.

"Come down you flicking liar! Get down from there. I'll cut your throat, I'll break every bone in your body!" After a pause there came a sharp click, as if he had pulled the trigger. Mannering stepped off the hatch for the first time as a bullet did strike and splinter it, had he still been standing on it, the bullet could have bruised if not broken his foot.

Then, came other sounds, particularly of car engines, roaring.

The hatch cover lifted an inch, then dropped into place. Car doors slammed and more engines raced.

Crammed in a corner of the attic was an old leather trunk, and Mannering stretched out and gripped it, finding it almost impossible to move. He dragged with both hands, until it was over the hatch, and as he dragged he saw the white lettering, faded and scratched but still quite readable. It said:

THOMAS FORRESTER
LETTS COLLEGE.
HERTS.

Down below Mannering there were thudding footsteps, but up here everything was still. In the far distance a man was shouting and raving: *could* that be Sangster? Mannering moved towards the roof window, and opened it. Gentle breezes blew. He hauled himself out but kept down low, creeping forward until he could see into the street. A big car had just pulled up, and a uniformed policeman opened the door.

Chief Inspector Willison climbed out, with Bristow behind him. It was as if Bristow had joined forces again with Scotland Yard.

Mannering edged further forward, lying flat on his stomach, concealed from the people in the street. It would not be long before some of the police began to push at the bathroom hatch but Mannering was held here by a compulsion he could not resist. He had to know what the men below were saying. He heard a man walk forward and say :

"Good morning, sir." That was alert Detective Sergeant Joslin.

"What's the latest?" Willison demanded.

"We've caught Bruce Sangster, and he's behaving like a lunatic. If he goes on like this we'll need a strait-jacket, sir."

"Not Mannering?"

"He's not been here, sir. The only other man seen was Forrester."

"Did you get him?"

Joslin said clearly : "No, sir. We caught the old man who lives downstairs, trying to get out the back way. His pockets were stuffed with rubies and emeralds —"

"The Fioras?" barked Willison.

"I should think so, sir, but I'm no judge of jewellery."

"Mr. Bristow here can look them over," Willison said, with great satisfaction. "What have you got on Sangster?"

"You've got enough on Sangster to know he's probably holding Lorna Mannering," Bristow rasped. "The Sangster place must be raided *now*." He was glaring at Willison, and Mannering could tell the depth of his emotions, the acuteness of his fear for Lorna.

Willison drew a deep breath, and then leaned into the car and gave instructions for a raid on Sir Gordon Sangster's house. When he had finished, he turned back to Joslin, and asked coldly :

"Well — what exactly have we got on Sangster?"

"He shot and wounded one of our men, sir. And he

carried a waist-belt obviously used for keeping the jewels in — two or three are still in it, sir, attached to a kind of self-adhesive felt. That's why he tried to get away, I should say. So there's little doubt they're our men."

"But *no* Mannering?" Willison asked, as if he couldn't believe that this was true. "Only Forrester, who—"

"Here *is* Forrester," Joslin exclaimed, and Mannering's heart seemed to jump a mile.

For Forrester was standing at the open door of a taxi which came from the Wandsworth Bridge Road direction. Mannering took a chance and peered over.

No one looked up. Instead, Bristow, Willison and Joslin lined up on the kerb, their backs to the houses. In the distance there was sound of Sangster's voice still ranting. Nearer, was a ring of policemen and old Fred, who was handcuffed to a young detective in plainclothes, and taken to a police car.

He stopped short, and stared at the real Forrester, and his voice came husky but clear.

"Well, Tom boy, they caught me red-handed. I know I'm an old rascal, but the time's come to tell the cops *you* only did whatever you did because Sangster blackmailed you. You'll be in the clear, Tom boy, don't you fret. And that's only one of the things I'll tell them when I turn Queen's Evidence . . ." He went on, as cunning and crafty as ever.

Forrester was out of the taxi, now, and saying :

"What's going on?" He glared at Bristow. "Why did you try to keep me away? Who the hell are you to think I can't handle my own affairs?"

"That's right, Tom boy," said old Fred. "Give it to them." He cackled with laughter. "It wasn't until your double shook the living daylight out of me that I realised you had a double. He really fooled me."

"Double !" exclaimed Joslin.

"Did you keep the real Forrester away?" Willison asked Bristow, his voice suddenly cold.

"Yes, I did. I'll go into details later," Bristow said. "The first task is to find Lorna Mannering. I want to go to Sangster's house."

In the silence which followed, while Willison was making up his mind how to respond, Sangster's ranting sounded nearer, the raving of a man who was out of his mind, who might have killed Lorna before he had left his home that day. Had Mannering known that he had been on a knife edge between sanity and madness he would never had taken the chance of waiting. If Lorna was dead — the fear was like a knife thrust in his breast.

Then the driver of the car which had brought Willison and Bristow leaned out of the open door.

"Message just in from *Information*, sir. Our chaps have found Mrs. Mannering in a room in Sir Gordon Sangster's house. Mrs. Sangster isn't there, sir. Will you —"

Willison was already moving towards the car, and Bristow was close behind him.

Mannering rolled over so that he could not be seen, relaxing while relief surged through him in enormous waves. After the shock ending of the suspense, he felt both weak and sick, but a few minutes later his heart was racing with exhilaration. He moved back further from the edge and crept across the roof-tops. Someone was thudding nearby, probably the police trying to open the attic hatch. He moved gingerly until he was a dozen houses away, and did exactly as he had when he had last been on these roofs. This time no one saw him; or at least, no one called out. He dropped into the service alley and ran to Wandsworth Bridge Road, near the shops. The parade was thronged with people but no one took any notice of him. He drove the long way round to the garage, sat in the car and cleaned off the greasepaint with pure alcohol kept in the garage for that purpose, loosened the gum and pulled off the extra hair. Looking much more like himself, he left the car in the garage and walked towards Chelsea.

A taxi came along, from behind him, and stopped at his call. He sat comfortably until they reached Green Street, where he paid off the taxi and went up to his own flat. No one was on the landing, no one was inside. He went up to the attic studio, took off the rest of the make-up, and then went down and changed into a dark suit. He had just finished, and for the first time relaxed completely, when there was a ring at the front door bell; next moment came the sound of a key in the lock. He was in the hall when the door opened and a policeman came in with Lorna only a pace behind him; and on the instant she saw Mannering.

She looked pale and tired but unhurt:

"John," she said. "Oh, John! Thank God!"

At Riston Street, Willison, who seemed aloof and almost hostile with Bristow, finished searching Number 17 and then went across to Number 20. When there was no answer, he had one of his men force a window, and climb in. Stiff and horrified, Paget was exactly where Mannering had left him. When he learned that both old Fred and Bruce Sangster were under arrest he began to talk freely.

He had been forced to do what he had, he claimed; he had been blackmailed, he hadn't had a chance . . .

"You'll have a chance to tell all that to a judge and jury," Willison said. He gave orders for this little house to be searched, and then went across to Number 17, where Bristow was in the downstairs front room, checking over the jewels. As if indifferent to Willison's coldness which verged on hostility, he looked up and nodded with satisfaction.

"Undoubtedly the Fioras," he pronounced. "Only two pieces missing, both of them rings, when we add these to the other lot. I suggested to Joslin that your chaps should search upstairs."

"And no doubt my chaps did exactly what you advised — as if they were your chaps. Bill —" Willison made the name sound as if it were chilled — "do you know who doubled for Tom Forrester?"

"No," Bristow replied.

"Can you guess?"

"Anyone can guess," Bristow retorted.

Willison said distantly. "I guess that it was Mannering. I've done a lot of guessing in the last day or two. Some people would call it deducing." Willison drew in his breath. "But for the impersonator we might never have caught the men we did. I'm beginning to see how you and he used to work together. Give him a message for me, will you?"

"Yes," Bristow said.

"Thank you. It's simply this. I don't propose to try to rake up the past. But if he ever becomes involved in criminal activity, no matter how good the motive, and if I can prove it, I'd handle him with no more leniency than I will Sangster."

The two men, Bristow so upright, grey-haired and clean-cut; Willison with his fair hair, fair eyebrows, almost colourless eyes, stared at each other; and Willison went on:

"Don't let him make any mistake, will you? And don't make any mistake yourself. A retired police officer would get less mercy from the law than anyone else."

Bristow said, very quietly: "I came to realise that some-times you get more justice if you bend the law. Think about that, will you?" There was a long silence between them, one which neither broke, for Tom Forrester came running down the stairs, angry as ever.

"Someone's stolen four of my self-portraits! *There's* something to get back, they're a damned sight more valu-able than a few odds and ends of jewellery!"

Bristow was taken aback.

Willison said coldly: "A witness, Clive Arnold Paget, has accused you of stealing certain artists materials, and of conspiring to pass off known fakes for signed old masters. I must ask you for a statement, Mr. Forrester."

Something in his glinting eyes stifled the protest on Forrester's lips.

By the time his statement was ready, including an ad-mission about the painting materials taken from an art school, but a denial of the rest, the police had begun a

thorough search of the treasure house in the strong room at
Sangster House. Bristow knew enough to be quite sure
that either Sangster or his son had been replacing genuine
works of art with copies, and building up fortunes in overseas banks. His wife, young and pretty, broke down under
questioning and explained why :

"His father had disowned him," she said. "They'd come
to hate each other. That —" there were tears in her eyes
as she went on : "That's the only reason Bruce didn't kill
him, why he had to keep him alive. Once he was dead,
all the treasures would go to museums and publicly owned
art galleries, and the substitutions would be found out."

Sangster himself, kept under opiates, was too ill to
speak, but it was soon obvious that his son learned that the
old man had acquired the Fioras knowing them to have
been stolen. Bruce in turn had stolen them, and tried to
find a market, but the ordinary fences were too nervous,
and Mannering had seemed just right. With good nursing
the old man began to recover, but even when he heard
what his son had done over the years he made no comment. It was as if he had cut Bruce not only out of his
will, but out of his mind. He did not live long enough to
be charged with possessing stolen jewels.

At the trial, Bruce Sangster was found guilty of murder
and sentenced to life imprisonment. Old Fred was given
five years imprisonment, which was for him 'life', for
attempted murder by using a fire-arm, and conspiracy
to dispose of jewels knowing them to be stolen. Paget was
sentenced to five years for his insurance frauds. Forrester,
who gave Queen's Evidence, was not charged, but he
became a central figure at the trial. As a result when the
first exhibitions of his paintings was held, hundreds stood
in line to visit, and little red 'sold' stickers soon began to
appear on picture after picture. There were some com-
plaints from the elderly, for the exhibition was held at
Riston Street.

"There isn't a better place to show just what they're
like," Lorna said to Tom Forrester.

"Oh, I agree," Forrester said, "but if only the young
nd physically fit can get upstairs, that's a damned shame.
Art belongs to everyone, not just to the few." He glared
as if accusingly at the Mannerings.

"John," Lorna turned to Mannering, who was by her
side, "isn't there some way of enabling everybody to go
upstairs?"

"I think we could put in a hoist, worked with a small
electric motor, or even by hand," Mannering answered.

After the third week, there was nothing left to sell, but
Forrester began to paint with furious haste, little gems
which he flung off as if they were sparks from a hammer
on an anvil. These sparks seemed to strike into Julie's eyes,
and make them radiant. She was here, there and everywhere, at the little house, although Forrester seemed to
take her no less for granted.

"Yet she couldn't be more happy," Lorna said, as they
left, one day towards the end of the exhibition. "I've a
feeling that he might make love to a thousand women,
but only be in love with her."

"The perfect husband," Mannering said straight-faced;
and a moment later the sparks began to fly from Lorna's
eyes. She was still looking at her radiant best when they
reached Quinns. There, Rupert Smith and young Armitage
were like Edwardian twins, each deeply immersed in a
customer's needs. Bristow was behind the carved partition,
examining some jewels with the help of a watchmaker's
glass.

Life was back to normal at the little shop of great
renown.

THE BARON SERIES IN CORONET

☐	12813 5	THE BARON IN FRANCE	20p
☐	15076 9	SALUTE FOR THE BARON	25p
☐	15077 7	DANGER FOR THE BARON	25p
☐	15113 7	NEST EGG FOR THE BARON	25p
☐	16042 X	THE BARON GOES EAST	25p
☐	16209 0	FRAME THE BARON	25p
☐	17316 5	A SWORD FOR THE BARON	25p
☐	02486 0	THE BARON GOES FAST	30p
☐	18306 3	BLACK FOR THE BARON	30p
☐	18305 5	SPORT FOR THE BARON	30p

All these books are available at your bookshop or newsagent, or can be ordered direct from the publisher. Just tick the titles you want and fill in the form below.

CORONET BOOKS, P.O. Box 11, Falmouth, Cornwall.
Please send cheque or postal order. No currency, and allow the following for postage and packing:
1 book – 10p, 2 books – 15p, 3 books – 20p, 4–5 books – 25p, 6–9 books – 4p per copy, 10–15 books – 2½p per copy, over 30 books free within the U.K.
Overseas – please allow 10p for the first book and 5p per copy for each additional book.

Name ....

Address ....

....